X802161255

7000354183

D1436492

TELEPEN

 University of the
West of England

BRISTOL

**EDUCATION
RESOURCES
CENTRE**

This book should be returned by the last date
stamped below.

UWE, BRISTOL   B1084.03.01
Printing & Stationery Services

2 8. NOV 2006

UWE BRISTOL
WITHDRAWN
LIBRARY SERVICES

Danish Fairy Tales

So many translations and adaptions of the works of Hans Andersen exist that to add yet another would be superfluous. It is fortunate, however, that the other vast store of Danish fairy and folk tales remains untapped and overlooked by English publishers. These are the stories which, unlike those of Andersen, who created his own, have been passed down from generation to generation by word of mouth.

As they worked together, spinning and knitting in their moorland homes, Danish peasants used to entertain each other with fairy tales that reflected their customs, hopes, fears and fantasies. A century ago, teachers and students travelled to all parts of the kingdom to take down each story direct from the narrator's mouth.

Since their publication in Denmark they have been an unfailing source of enjoyment to Danish children, and the stories – fresh, vigorous and varied – which are now retold and beautifully illustrated in this volume, will undoubtedly prove equally popular with English children.

Danish Fairy Tales

Retold by
INGE HACK

Illustrated by
HARRY AND ILSE TOOTHILL

FREDERICK MULLER LIMITED
LONDON

First published in Great Britain 1964
by Frederick Muller Limited
Printed and bound by
Cox & Wyman Ltd., London, Fakenham and Reading

COPYRIGHT © 1964 BY INGE HACK

REPRINTED 1965

Folk tales
Fairy tales
of
Denmark

YF

REDLAND COLLEGE
REDLAND HILL
BRISTOL
BS6 6UZ
29605

To
ANTON

Contents

Illustrations

Introduction

HARDLY A YEAR passes without the publication of a new edition of Fairy Tales by Hans Christian Andersen, and publishers and authors vie with each other in an attempt to produce an improved translation or a better selection. In so doing they overlook the other vast reservoir of Danish fairy stories – stories which, unlike those of Andersen, who created his own, have been passed down through the centuries by word of mouth. These are the tales I have sought and which are retold in this volume.

Danish peasants – men and women – once knitted stockings for their livelihood, and as they worked together in their moorland homes they entertained each other with fairy tales through which their outlook on life and their customs still live on. To the child of today these customs may seem as strange as they were familiar and homely to the original story-tellers. Much of what now appears fantasy was then reality; witches and trolls, mermen and devils were seen as something real or as something embedded in an ancient faith reaching far back into the Dark Ages.

The cattle-dealers who drove their herds southwards to the great markets of Schleswig, the potters who journeyed deep into Germany to trade their wares and the soldiers who were stationed in Holstein had many opportunities of listening to German fairy stories; and perhaps it is this influence that accounts for the gruesomeness of some of the Danish tales. 'Peder Okse' and 'The Fisherman's Son' testify to these times. Some stories bear the stamp of history: the introduction of

'King Find's Daughter' reflects the impressions of the Danish–English Seven Years War (1807–14).

In the eighteenth century the Danish upper classes despised fairy tales, and when general education was introduced in Denmark in 1814 it was considered the height of stupidity to tell such stories. Children were expected to think, speak and behave as adults. But the peasants clung to their fairy tales, which were thus preserved for a more enlightened age.

A century ago Grundtvig and Berntsen made the first serious attempt to tap Denmark's wealth of fairy and folk tales, and students and teachers travelled to all parts of the kingdom to write down each story direct from the narrator's mouth. Since their publication they have given endless pleasure to young people in Denmark, and it is hoped that these stories will now provide a source of enjoyment and enrichment for English children, too.

Inge Hack

Redditch, March 1963

ONE

The Fisherman's Son

A FISHERMAN and his son once sailed on the Lim Fjord. They had fished for a whole day and night with little luck and had just decided to return home when they saw another boat speeding towards them. The strange boat drew up alongside theirs and they were surprised to see a woman at the helm. 'If only I could have your lovely little boy,' she sighed, 'I would reward you well.' The fisherman shook his head. 'No, my children are not for sale. Besides, this is my eldest son and one day, God willing, he will have to keep us old ones and his little brothers and sisters,' he replied. The woman persisted, however, and promised the fisherman that if he would part with his little boy, he would find a hundredweight of golden coins on his table when he arrived home; as for his child, she would love and care for him as if he were her own. The fisherman thought deeply. Never in his whole life had he seen a hundredweight of golden coins, let alone owned them. Eventually his craving for wealth proved stronger than his love for his son. 'All right,' he agreed; 'if you will take good care of him you may have him.' Wide-eyed with fear, the little boy struggled hard to hold back his tears. He had always been his father's favourite child and now he was being given away by the one who loved him. 'Shall I never be able to go home again?' he stammered. 'Of course,' replied the woman. 'If you are a good boy I shall take you home for a few days.' Reassured by this news, the boy said good-bye to his father and clambered into the woman's boat which disappeared into the mist. When the fisherman returned home he told his anxious wife of the bargain he had made with the strange woman, and there, sure enough, on the table he found a hundred-weight of golden coins.

On the opposite shore of the fjord the woman lifted the boat over her shoulder, caught hold of the boy's hand and led him across the moors. Eventually they came to another lake, and as soon as they had crossed it, off she went holding the boy's hand and with the boat on her shoulder. Thus they travelled until evening, leaving lake after lake behind them. Finally the journey ended. There, near the water's edge, stood an ancient castle, and behind it were the remains of a withered forest where no birds sang and no flowers grew. Everything was forlorn and desolate. The woman took the boy's hand and led him past countless broken bricks and huge stones until they came to an underground passage. Through the entrance they went and into a room with thick carpets and velvet curtains, beautifully-carved chairs and a snowy-white bed.

Darkness fell swiftly. The woman went out and the boy climbed into the soft bed. Although he was warm and comfortable, he could not sleep; instead he thought of the home he had left behind him. His mind was still wandering when a noise by the door disturbed him and someone entered, but who or what it was he could not tell. A shudder ran down his spine as the silent figure crept into bed with him. The boy was very frightened and lay quite still, but as time went by and nothing happened, he felt with his hand in the dark where the strange creature lay. It was a human face he touched, and when he moved his feet he brushed against the slippery tail of a fish.

Eventually he fell asleep, and as soon as he awoke next morning he turned his head; but the strange creature had gone. At once he jumped out of bed and was surprised to find in place of the ragged clothes he had left on the chair a new suit of the very finest material. He would look just like a prince in these fine clothes, he thought. He had just dressed when the woman came in with his breakfast, and after he had eaten she gave him a magic mirror in which he could see his home and his family and all they were doing. The little mirror helped him through his sad moments, and whenever time dragged he always fetched it from his drawer and home came back to him.

Every night after dark the strange creature came into his bed and every morning before daylight it disappeared; but as it never caused him any harm he learnt to take no notice of it. During the daytime the woman washed him and fed him and spoke lovingly to him.

One day, three years later, the woman asked him if he would like to go home. His eyes sparkled with delight. He could go, she said, if he promised to do exactly as she bade him. During the three days he would stay at home he was to obey his father, but not his mother; and on the third day when he heard a shot he was to pack his clothes together. Then a second shot would ring out and he was to leave home, but without a candle or matches. Finally he would hear a third shot and he was to make his way at once to the side of the fjord on which they had met. The boy gave his word to do exactly as the woman had told him, and as dusk was falling she took him over lake and land to his moorland home.

In the meantime the boy's father still fished every day on the Lim Fjord, but now he was alone. He often thought wistfully of the hours he and his son used to spend together, but so long had passed since they had heard from him that he and his wife had given up all hope of ever seeing him again. Thus their joy was great when the boy opened the door of their cottage; and the lantern glowed long past midnight as his parents, brothers and sisters sat spellbound, listening to all that had happened to him. They all squirmed when he told them of his strange bed-companion with a fish's tail, and his mother said she would pack candles and matches for him to take back. 'No!' declared his father, 'the kind woman is looking after him well and we must not risk offending her.' When the boy was alone with his mother, however, she gave him an old tinder-box. 'This will give him enough light to see who is lying beside him,' she thought, 'and he is not disobeying the woman.'

Exactly at noon on the third day a shot echoed down the Lim Fjord and at once the boy collected his belongings. On the second shot he said good-bye to his mother, brothers and sisters, and his father accompanied him down to the boat where the woman sat waiting for him. By the time the third shot rang out the boy was already in the boat, and with a final wave to the fisherman, they sailed off across the fjord.

The journey was long and tedious, and when at last they reached the old palace the boy's eyes were drooping. He went straight to bed with his tinder-box hidden under his pillow. How long he slept he could not tell, but he awoke to find the strange creature beside him and sound asleep. He reached for his tinder-box and struck a light. As the glow fell upon his bed-companion he saw with amazement the face of the woman who looked after him every day. Her eyelids flickered and she opened her eyes. Then she burst out crying for now, she said, her happiness was gone; never again would she be able to sleep with the boy. She was a princess, she sobbed, under the power of a wicked troll who had killed her father and all her family, burnt down their palace and made her his slave. The troll had only allowed her to have the little boy as a companion on condition that no light was ever struck, for lights are what all trolls fear. Now she had disobeyed him, the boy would be taken away from her and she would have to spend all her days alone with the troll.

The princess was now so upset that the boy reproached himself and wished with all his heart that he could right the wrong he had done her. 'There must be something we can do,' he said at last. 'Can't we kill this wicked troll?' She shook her head sadly. 'If only you were as big and strong as he, there would be hope,' she sighed, and went on to tell the boy that the troll once told her of the only way he could be killed. 'Only if he is hit on top of the head with a certain egg will he die,' she said; 'but this egg is kept in a deep forest in Germany in the safe-keeping of his brother-troll who is much more evil and savage. Even if you were to kill this troll he would change into a dragon, and if the dragon were killed there would appear a stag; and if you managed to catch and slay the stag a dove would fly off high into the sky. It is only when you kill this dove that his brother's power is broken; and inside the dove you will find the egg.' 'Then I shall find and kill the troll's brother or die in the attempt,' vowed the boy.

The boy rose before dawn, but when he went to where he had laid his fine suit he found in its place his old ragged clothes, now so tight that he could only just squeeze into them. Quietly he crept outside and was well on his way before the troll realized he had gone. For many days he walked across the heath of Jutland until one morning he saw a lion, a dog and a falcon, all quarrelling over the carcass of an ox which lay by the wayside. Hoping they had not noticed him, he turned on his heel, and with his heart in his mouth hurried on by a roundabout way. Unfortunately, the lion had seen him and asked the falcon to fetch the boy so that he could settle their dispute. Hearing the flapping of wings, the boy looked up and saw the falcon flying towards him. He was terrified, thinking the bird would tear him apart; but when he found out what was required of him he heaved a great sigh of relief. In fact, both the animals and the bird seemed very friendly and asked him to share the carcass among them. The boy thought for a few moments and then decided that the lion should have the ox's flesh, the dog its bones and the falcon its insides. This arrangement satisfied all of them, and so pleased was the lion that, as a reward, he gave the boy power to change himself, whenever he wished, into a lion ten times stronger and fiercer than he himself was. The dog promised that, whenever he wished, the boy could become a dog ten times as swift as himself. Finally, the falcon said that, as often as he wished, the boy could turn into a bird like himself only ten times bigger and faster.

Very pleased with his reward, the boy thanked them all and went on his way. Towards the end of the day he felt very weary and made a wish. At once he turned into a falcon and with powerful flaps of his wings he flew swiftly through the air, mile after mile falling back behind him. On and on he sped over the land and into Germany until below him he saw a magnificent castle. It was here in the surrounding forest that the troll roamed. He glided to earth and having settled on the ground, he made a wish. Immediately he was a boy once more.

Up to the castle he went and asked if he could be

taken into the King's service. Wearing a worried look, the King thought for a few moments. 'Yes, I certainly do need a smart lad to look after my herd, but I must warn you that if any goats wander off into the forest at the far end of my field you will never set eyes on them again, for the troll will steal them.' The boy promised to take every care of the animals and the King took him into service, although so far no one had ever been able to protect his goats from the troll.

Early the next morning the boy drove the herd across the field and into the forest. Almost at once he heard a terrifying yell and the wicked troll rushed towards him, shouting, 'These goats will do nicely for my dinner. Now off you go back to the castle and leave the herd with me, otherwise I'll gobble you up as well.' The boy stood his ground. 'No,' he replied firmly. 'You won't get so much as the smallest kid while I'm in charge of the King's herd.' So saying, he made a wish, and in the form of a lion he charged at the troll. The battle lasted most of the morning with the fur flying all around them until exhaustion made them both loosen their grip. 'If only I'd had a goat inside me it wouldn't have taken me long to have finished you off,' boasted the troll. 'And if only I'd had a bottle of wine from the King's cellar you would be no more,' answered the boy. With this the troll went off deep into the forest while the boy walked home with his herd.

Awaiting him at the castle gate was the King who was both happy and amazed to find that not a single goat had been lost. He inquired how the boy had fared and learnt that everything had gone well. However, the King was puzzled and the following day he commanded one of his servants to find out how the boy managed to save the animals from the troll. The next evening the excited servant came racing back to the castle and told

'These goats will do

his story. There had been a dreadful struggle between the troll and a lion with hairs and fur flying all over the place, he said, and when they were both almost too weak to stand, he heard the lion gasp, 'If only I'd had a bottle of wine from the King's cellar, I'd have finished off the troll.' 'Very well,' declared the King, 'the lion shall have it,' and the following day the servant carried a bottle of wine in his pocket in case he saw them fighting again.

Some time after the return of the servant the boy came home with his herd. Again the King received him joyfully and tried to find out what had happened; but beyond saying that everything had gone well the boy revealed nothing.

On the third morning the boy went off again with his herd, and behind him followed the servant with a bottle of wine from the King's cellar. Immediately the troll came rushing towards them, demanding a goat for his breakfast and threatening that if the boy refused, he

nicely for my dinner.'

would take the whole herd and him as well. The boy
replied that the troll would only take a goat over his
dead body, and wishing himself into a lion he made
straight for his enemy. They clawed and scratched and
pulled and snapped all day long until the sun went
down. At last the troll cried, 'If only I had three goats
inside me I would soon put paid to you.' 'If only I had a
bottle of wine from the King's cellar you would not live
to see tomorrow,' retorted the boy. On hearing these
words, the King's servant dashed up to the lion and
gave him the wine just as the troll had decided to go.
The lion drained the bottle and his strength returned.
Then, with a mighty spring, he landed on the troll's back
and tore him to pieces. But the troll was not finished,
and out of his skin emerged a dragon which the lion immediately pounced upon and pulled to bits. In place of
the dragon a fleet-footed stag darted along the road. At
once the boy wished he were a dog and then bounded
off in pursuit. The stag was soon caught and torn to

pieces. The troll now changed into a dove and soared
high into the sky. In reply the boy made another wish
and, as a huge falcon, he soon overtook the dove and
pecked it to pieces; and with the dead bird in its talons
the falcon floated back to earth. Here the boy wished he
could become himself again and soon he had found the
egg inside the dove.

Triumphantly the boy drove the herd back to the
castle and told the King that the troll was dead, and
since from now on it would be an easy job to look after
the animals, he asked if he might go back home. The
King was very reluctant to lose him, but seeing that the
boy was longing for his own people and country, he
finally consented.

At once the boy made a wish and, as a falcon, he flew
back to the princess as fast as his wings would carry him.
No doubt the princess was hoping for his return and her
freedom. At long last he reached the ruined palace and
saw that the princess was busy combing the troll's hair
with a steel comb. She had heard the flapping of wings
and turned to see the huge falcon settle on the palace
ruins. That was strange, she thought, for never before
had a bird settled there. She immediately asked the
troll's permission to try to catch it, and when he consented, she crept stealthily up to the falcon; but the bird
sat quite still, and just as she was going to pounce on it
there stood before her the fisherman's son in his ragged
clothes. She flung her arms around his neck and the troll
became so jealous that he ordered the boy to leave for
good.

Not long afterwards the princess saw the same falcon
perched in exactly the same place as before. So beautifully did the bird sing that the princess pleaded with the
troll to let her fetch it inside. She knew full well that it
was really the little boy and begged to be allowed to

keep him with her. The troll refused, but she pestered so much that at last, for the sake of peace, he gave in to her. Joyfully the princess ran after the falcon and as soon as she had it in her hands, the fisherman's son appeared again.

Immediately the boy ran to his room and looked into the mirror, for he was anxious to find out how his parents, brothers and sisters were at home. Happily all was well.

Later on in the evening he was left alone with the princess and then he told her of his adventures in Germany. Her excitement grew, and when he handed her the egg she jumped for joy at the thought of escaping from the troll's web and the spell in which her father's palace had been held for so long.

The following morning, as usual, she washed and combed the troll's hair. That day he was very haughty and told her again that nobody could ever take her away from him, for even the bravest in the land dare not fight his brother for the egg. Then, very satisfied with himself, the vain troll showed the princess the place where the egg must strike if it were to kill him. In a flash the princess raised her hand and brought it down on the troll's head, and he fell dead on the spot. At the very same moment a mighty roar filled the air and the princess found herself in her former home, as magnificent and stately as before. Now she had been released from the troll's web and was her real self again. She immediately freed her family and many others who had fallen under the power of the troll.

Out in the forest the beech-trees were fresh and green and the birds sang as never before. The King, Queen, and all their people were happy again, but their joy became even greater when the princess fetched the poor fisherman's boy and told them that it was he who had saved them all. She kissed him in front of everyone and, with her father's blessing, said she intended to marry him. Then the beautiful princess attired the boy in royal clothes and that same day they celebrated their wedding; and for many, many years they lived happily together.

TWO

Graadonner

LONG AGO IN Denmark there lived two Lords of the Manor. One of them was young but the other, who had a beautiful daughter, was getting on in years. Each Lord had his own manor, but as they were close friends they often used to ride the dozen or so miles between their two estates to visit each other; sometimes, however, they would sail across the lake on either side of which their two homes lay.

As you can imagine, there came many suitors to the daughter of the old Lord of the Manor, but she showed not the slightest interest in them. She always remained in her attic and allowed them to make fools of themselves. One day, thinking he might succeed where the others had all failed, the young Lord of the Manor decided to woo her. He made careful preparations, and with four snowy-white horses in front of his carriage he set off. Although the old Lord of the Manor would have been delighted to have his young friend as a son-in-law, his daughter showed no enthusiasm at all, and was only keen on getting up into the attic. However, she was obliged to come downstairs at dinner-time, but scarcely had she finished eating when she dashed out into the kitchen and asked her servants to cut off the tails and manes of the four white horses and to cover them all over in dirt. Then she hurried back up to her attic and not a soul saw her for the rest of that day. In the evening, when the young Lord of the Manor was about to return home, his coachman discovered the horses in a dreadful state. Their fine tails and manes had been cut off, and so completely covered in dirt were they that no one could recognize them. The young Lord became very despondent, but nothing could be done about it for he knew who was responsible. All he wanted to do was to get home as soon as he could, hoping no one would notice him. Then he intended to give the horses to the

With four snowy-white horses in

serfs for he would never be able to drive out with them again.

Now, try as he might, the young Lord of the Manor could not forget the beautiful girl, and not many days passed before he felt that he had to visit her again. This time, thinking they looked finer, he used four shining black horses to pull his carriage. He soon reached his friend's home and the old Lord was pleased to welcome him. But, as before, his daughter stayed in the attic, and not until a message was sent up to her did she come down for dinner. As before, she finished eating and then dashed out to the servants, asking them to cut off the tails and manes of the horses and to smear them with cream. This made the young Lord more downhearted than ever and he hurried home, taking all the loneliest roads so that no one should see him. He was unable to use his black horses again and gave these to the serfs, too.

Having now received two setbacks, the young Lord decided against driving to his friend's daughter. He would try sailing instead. He bought a beautiful boat and set off across the lake. But high up in her attic the

ront of his carriage he set off.

old Lord's daughter saw him coming and made her plans. As soon as they had eaten, she ran out to the kitchen and told her servants to bore holes all over the boat. Then she hurried back to her attic and no one saw any more of her the rest of that day. In the evening when the young Lord decided to return home, he found that his boat was full of water. He knew who the culprit was, but could do nothing about it. So he had to go home on foot.

Now half-way between the two manors the young Lord owned a mill, and, feeling tired and sad, he decided to stay there the night. The miller's wife noticed

how downcast he looked and asked him what had gone
wrong. The young Lord confided his troubles in her,
telling how he had failed three times to win the old
Lord's daughter. He loved her so much, he added, that
he couldn't live without her. Although only a humble
woman, the miller's wife was very wise and gave him
some good advice. The young Lord listened intently and
early next morning completed his journey, determined
to do what the miller's wife had told him.

As soon as he reached home the young Lord of the
Manor bought a golden spinning-wheel, a golden spindle
and a golden spinning-tree. He then dressed himself in
an old grey smock, a greasy hat and a pair of worn-out
clogs. In that attire, in the late afternoon, he made
his way towards the old Lord's estate. Now it happened
that the old Lord and his wife were not at home, for
they had decided to spend a few days with some friends
who lived on the other side of the wood. Pretending to
be an old, sick beggar, the young Lord asked the head
cowman whether he might spend the night in the byres.
The cowman took pity on him and gave him shelter.
Next morning the young Lord had breakfast with all the
farm labourers, and after eating he said to the cowman,
'Listen. As you were kind enough to give me shelter last
night, I will drive your cattle to the water for you.' The
cowman accepted his offer, so the beggar drove the
cattle down to the lake, using his golden spinning-wheel
to chase them with. Meanwhile, up in the attic, the
young maiden saw the old beggar with his golden spinning-wheel. 'That golden spinning-wheel I must have,'
she thought to herself, and sent out one of her servants to
fetch the beggar. 'The maiden wishes to speak to you,'
said the servant, 'and she wants you to bring what you
used to chase the cattle with.' Carrying his golden

spinning-wheel under his arm, the beggar went back to
the manor house and up the stairs to the attic. 'What do
you want for your spinning-wheel?' the maiden demanded. 'I don't want to sell it,' replied the beggar. 'I
will give you all the money you need,' she said. 'That
makes no difference at all,' said the beggar. 'I don't
need any money, so I don't intend to sell. Well, yes,' he
went on, after thinking hard for a few moments, 'if I
may sit just outside your bedroom door for one night,
then you may have it.' 'No, that will never do to have
you, old Graadonner, sitting there.' 'Don't worry little
maiden,' reassured the servants; 'it won't hurt to have
him outside your room, for we shall be close by, and if
anything is the matter you have only to call us.' Now so
badly did the maiden want the golden spinning-wheel
that she gave permission for the old beggar to sit outside her door the following night, but on two conditions:
that he didn't go up to her room until after everyone
had gone to bed and that he left very early the following
morning before anyone had got up. This the old beggar
gladly promised. It was not long before darkness fell,
and when all was quiet, he crept upstairs and settled
down outside the maiden's door, keeping as quiet as a
mouse. Inside, however, the old Lord's daughter turned
and twisted and didn't sleep a wink; all night she kept
thinking of the nasty, grey-haired little man outside her
room. Very early the next morning before anyone was
about, the beggar tiptoed downstairs.

He again drove the cattle to the water after breakfast,
but he had retained the golden spindle, and this he used
to chase the animals. The maiden up in the attic had
noticed that the spindle of the golden spinning-wheel
was missing, and seeing Graadonner with it, she sent
her servants for the old grey-haired man and asked him

to sell it. 'No, you can't have that,' said the beggar, 'unless you will allow me to sit outside your door one more night.' 'No, that won't possibly do. I can't have you, old Graadonner, sitting there again. Not a wink did I get last night because of you,' replied the maiden. 'What does it matter, little maiden?' interrupted the servants. 'If you need us you have only to call.' 'All right,' she agreed at last, 'I must have the spindle for my golden spinning-wheel, so I shall just have to put up with it. But don't forget, you must come late and go early as you did yesterday.' The maiden didn't sleep that night either, even though the old man sat as quiet as a mouse. But at daybreak he was gone.

The following morning the maiden saw that, as usual, the beggar was driving the cattle to the water, but this time he had with him the golden spinning-tree. She was determined to have that, too, and immediately sent for him. 'What do you want for your spinning-tree?' she asked. 'I will not sell it unless I can sit by your bed for one night,' replied the beggar. The maiden cried and groaned, for the nasty old man had ruined her sleep for two nights already. So badly did she want the spinning-tree, however, that in the end, her maids having promised to be near, she agreed. It was very late when old Graadonner came to her room and sat on the bed, as quiet as a mouse.

Now that same night the old Lord of the Manor and his wife returned home. Hearing their arrival below him, Graadonner threw the eiderdown over him and hammered heavily on the floor with his clogs. He made such a noise that the old Lord came upstairs to see what was the matter, and when he found the nasty, grey-haired little man in bed with his daughter he became furious. He reached for his whip and started beating both of them with all his might. His daughter screamed and yelled but of no avail. 'I don't want to set eyes on you ever again,' he cried, and chased both of them out of his house and off his estate.

Now when they had travelled a good distance from the old Lord's castle, the old beggar pretended that he didn't care for the beautiful maiden, whereupon she wrung her hands and cried, 'My dear Graadonner, please don't leave me.' 'Ah, well,' he replied, 'I can't have anything to do with you anyhow, for I work on the manor a few miles from here, and the Lord there is a nasty fellow; he certainly won't be in a good humour when he sees me come home with a woman.' The maiden begged and cried so pitifully, however, for now, she said, there was no place where she could stay. Finally, to her great relief, Graadonner was persuaded to take her – and this was just as he had planned it. So, with the maiden at his side, he set off towards his own manor. At last they reached his estate and there, out in the courtyard, stood a tiny, tumbledown house. 'This is where I live,' said Graadonner, pointing to it. 'If you want to be with me you will have to live in here.' When she saw what a miserable place it was, the maiden wept, but it was no use crying; she had to live here or nowhere. 'Tomorrow the servants bake the bread,' said Graadonner, 'so you must go and help them, otherwise the Lord of the Manor won't let you stay here. Now when you go up to the manor house I want you to steal some of the Lord's flour and put it in this little bag, for we must bake bread for ourselves later on this evening.' 'Oh, no,' she sobbed, 'I've never baked before and I couldn't possibly steal.' 'Oh, yes, you can,' he replied. 'If you don't, we shall both starve.'

Early the following morning Graadonner left the little house and soon afterwards the maiden went up to the manor to help bake the bread. At the door she met none other than the Lord of the Manor. 'Whoever are you?' he demanded, looking her up and down. 'I am Graadonner's wife,' she replied meekly. 'So he has got himself a woman to contend with now,' said the Lord of the Manor, adding severely, 'off you go and help my servants, and mind you pull your weight or you'll be shown the door!' Then off he went, and she felt relieved he had gone. But before leaving, the young Lord of the Manor had told his servants that occasionally they were to go outside and leave the new maid alone. Thus, when no one was about, she hastily stole the flour and filled the bag. After a long, hard day she got ready to return to her little home and Graadonner. Just as she was going out of the kitchen, however, in strode the Lord of the Manor, and spoke very harshly to her. 'You're a lazy wench! You haven't even earned your keep!' he cried, and shook her so violently that she dropped the bag and the flour spilt all over the floor. 'On top of that you're a thief, too,' he shouted. The maiden cried bitterly and begged of her master to let her go, promising never to steal again. The young Lord released his hold of her and back she went to her poor house as best she could.

Shortly afterwards Graadonner arrived. 'Well, did you get the flour?' he asked. At this the maiden burst into tears and told him how badly things had gone for her. Graadonner seemed very annoyed at first, but when he had calmed down he said, 'You must try to do better next time. Tomorrow is washing day and you must go and help the maids. When you have a chance, see whether you can steal a few clothes, for if we have little ones sometime we shall need them.' Again she cried, but it was no good protesting, she just had to obey. As on the previous day the other maids disappeared, and when she was alone she seized the opportunity to tuck pieces of clothing down her dress. When all the work was done and she was ready to go home, however, the Lord of the Manor appeared on the scene. He thought she looked rather plump, and asked what she was hiding underneath her dress. With tears in her eyes she admitted everything and received a good scolding from her master whose servants chased her back to her poor hut. Then Graadonner came in. Crying bitterly, she ran up to him and told him that she had been unlucky again. 'Well, if you can't do any better than that, you're not much use to me,' he cried. 'However,' he added, 'some sewing maids are coming tomorrow to make a wedding dress, for the Lord of the Manor is getting married. But his bride comes from a long way off and as you are the same size as she, the dress has to be tried on you. Now while you are doing this, see whether you can get hold of a few pieces of material, for they would come in very useful if we were to have babies.'

Next day the maiden went up to the manor where the fine wedding dress was tried on her. While dressing and undressing she managed to steal some material, and she was just tiptoeing off with it when, as luck would have it, the Lord of the Manor noticed her. He snatched the material from her, threatened to have her whipped and ordered her out of his house.

When Graadonner came home he told her that the Lord of the Manor was getting married on the following day. 'But,' he added, 'unfortunately his bride has fallen ill, so you will have to go to church and get married in her place.' She cried and cried, promising to do anything for Graadonner but this, and pleaded with him to let her off, for she was so afraid of the Lord of the Manor. 'It's no use moaning and groaning,' interrupted Graadonner; 'whatever the Lord of the Manor says must be obeyed.'

The next morning when they were due to start off,

c

Graadonner was suddenly taken ill. This made her very sad and now she didn't want to leave him. 'Never mind about me,' said Graadonner; 'you must go otherwise the master will become very angry, and might even get rid of us.' So, very unhappily, she went off to the manor. As soon as she was out of the door Graadonner had a good laugh to himself, and it wasn't long before he had taken his dirty old rags off and put on his fine bridegroom's clothes.

Now the Lord of the Manor ordered his servants to set fire to Graadonner's house at exactly the same time as he and the maiden set out from the manor for church, for he wanted to see what she would do. They were just getting inside the carriage when the hut went up in flames. 'Oh, my poor Graadonner!' she cried. 'Save him! He's ill and can't walk. Save him, please!' 'Oh, never mind about Graadonner,' shouted the Lord, 'he's not much use to us anyway. Now hurry up and get into the coach.' The maiden cried and cried over her poor Graadonner for he was so very ill, and now he would be burnt to death. But the Lord of the Manor refused to listen to her; they had to be off at once, he said, or they would be late for the service. Besides, he looked so wickedly at her that she daren't say another word.

All the maiden could think about during the wedding ceremony was her poor Graadonner, and when she returned from the church she glanced in the direction of the hut, but all she saw was a charred heap of rubble. Once they were inside the manor the young Lord suddenly turned to her and asked if she would like to see Graadonner again. Astonished, she replied that she would love to, but thought it impossible. The Lord of the Manor then fetched his old clothes from the bedroom and put them on. The beautiful girl now realized what had happened and she flung her arms around his neck and wept for joy. Visitors and guests from near and far were immediately invited to the manor, and the wedding was celebrated for several days. And when all the festivities had ended, the young maiden drove home to her parents who were overjoyed to see their daughter again. The young Lord of the Manor and his lady live in happiness and splendour to this very day.

Haltefanden (The Lame Devil)

ONCE UPON A time in Hjørring there lived a poor man. He was a postman and delivered letters and parcels between Hjørring and Løkken near the Western Sea.* As he was out on his post-round one day he was very worried, for his wife was expecting her baby at any moment. He hurried as much as he could, not wanting to be away from home too long. But that day, as luck would have it, his bag was heavier than usual and darkness had already fallen when he started back to Hjørring. At last he could see the lights of the town twinkling in the distance. Abruptly he stopped, for it seemed to him as though Hjørring was completely surrounded by a lake. He tried first one way, then another, but everywhere he saw water in front of him and couldn't find where to cross it. All this time he grew more and more anxious for his wife. Then he saw someone limping towards him. It was Haltefanden, the lame devil. 'Are you trying to find your way home?' inquired Haltefanden. 'I certainly am,' replied the postman; 'my wife is expecting our first child.' 'Then you will be pleased to hear that your wife has already given birth to a healthy boy,' said Haltefanden, 'but she is so disappointed you have not returned. Now if you will promise

* Western Sea = North Sea.

faithfully to give me the first one you see when you get home, then I'll immediately take you over the lake.'

Hearing this news, the postman longed even more for home and thought to himself, 'Let me think, who is the first to greet me when I arrive home? Why, of course, it's our little dog, and I'd sooner give him away than walk about here all night.' Then, looking at Haltefanden, he said, 'All right, it's a deal, but hurry up, I want to get home!'

Haltefanden at once lifted the postman on to his shoulders and hobbled off with him. There was no water at all; it was just an illusion. They soon reached the man's front door and here Haltefanden set him down on the step. The lame devil then took a sheet of paper from his pocket and said, 'The first to meet you will be your first-born son. When the boy is handed to you, take a needle and prick his right hand. Let three drops of blood fall on this paper; then bring it out to me! That shall be the pact between us. Do this and I won't demand your son until he is thirty years old.'

The poor man now felt sick at heart. Nervously he opened the door, and no sooner had he stepped inside than the midwife handed him his tiny son. He was so frightened of Haltefanden that he hastened to do what the lame devil had told him. He pricked the baby's hand with a needle, collected three drops of blood on the paper and gave the pact to Haltefanden. In a flash the lame devil was gone.

There never was a healthier child than the postman's son, and as he grew up he read widely and became quite scholarly. His talents did not go unnoticed, for the Provost of Hjørring took a kindly interest in the boy and kept him to his books, hoping that one day he would become a priest. Now while he was studying, the boy

could only visit his parents occasionally, but whenever
he went home his father always burst into tears.

The boy passed all his examinations with the highest
marks and then he travelled abroad to the great centres
of learning. Afterwards he returned to Denmark, intending to train as a priest. But first he had a duty to
return to Hjørring to thank the Provost for his help and
encouragement and to see his parents. Again, as soon as
he set eyes on him, his father broke down and cried. His
son could stand it no more and so he asked why his
father always cried when he returned to see them, for as
far as he was aware he had not caused them any sorrow.

'Very well, my boy,' his father said at last. 'Until now
only I have known your fate, but the time has come
when you must hear what is to happen to you.' He told
of his meeting many years before with Haltefanden, the
lame devil, and of all that had taken place. 'But why
haven't you told me before, Father?' demanded the boy.
'There are now only three days to go before Haltefanden comes for me. However, I don't intend to wait
for him. I'm going at once, and if I don't come back
before a week has passed, then you mustn't expect to see
me again.'

Out he went and across the fields. It was harvest
time, and as far as the eye could see there stretched the
yellow rye. He picked three ears of it and made his way
towards the nearest church. Here he dipped the three
ears of rye into the font and hid them safely in his purse.
He said a prayer, and went outside; then, after he had
cut an oak stick, he set off on his journey.

When darkness fell the young student found himself
in the middle of a wood, and seeing a small hut he went
up to it and knocked. The door was opened by an old
grey-bearded man who cried, 'How dare you come to
my home? If you know what is good for you, you will

be on your way as fast as you can, for this is a thieves' hide-out. My twelve grown sons are all thieves, and luckily for you they are not here. They will be home soon, however, and will kill you if they find you here. As for me, my days of thieving are over for I am old, and besides, I've done enough wickedness in my time. Now be off with you before it's too late!' 'But are you not preparing yourself for heaven?' inquired the student. 'No,' answered the old man, 'there isn't enough time for me to win a place there, but I've been promised the best bed in hell when my time comes. And may I ask you where you are going at this time of night?' 'I'm going to hell,' replied the student, 'but I'm hoping I won't be there long, so I'll call on the way back and tell you what they consider the best bed in hell.' Seeing the puzzled look on the old man's face, the student told him briefly the reason for his journey. Then he continued on his way.

Although the path was crooked, the student had no difficulty in finding his way and walked straight up to the gates of hell. He knocked boldly and waited. The gates were soon opened, and the person who welcomed him was none other than Haltefanden, the lame devil, who immediately recognized him. 'You have arrived early!' exclaimed Haltefanden. 'We didn't expect you until tomorrow.' The student didn't answer but went straight up to the oldest of the devils who was in chains and demanded the pact which his father had given to Haltefanden. The old one refused, saying, 'Whatever has entered the gates of hell will never come out again.' At this the student got out his purse, took one of the ears of rye and started knocking the old one with it.

The old devil screamed to Haltefanden to bring the pact, but the lame devil hid himself and would not answer. Then the student took the second ear of rye from his purse and struck the old devil with it. The old one winced with pain and yelled worse than before for Haltefanden to bring the pact. Still the lame devil refused. But the old devil had many trusted servants and these he summoned to help him. He ordered them to cast Haltefanden into cave after cave, each more terrifying than the previous one, until he obeyed. Their efforts were of no avail, however, for Haltefanden would not surrender the pact; the student, he said, was a learned man and, once he had the pact and was out of their power, he could cause them great harm in hell by winning over a good many souls for heaven.

Then the student took his third ear of rye and started beating the old devil harder than ever. The old one jumped and writhed and screamed and finally shouted to his servants to torture Haltefanden until he produced the pact; but it was of no use. In desperation the old devil in chains commanded his faithful angels to put Haltefanden into their best bed – Midian's bed. That did the trick. When he heard what was to happen to him, Haltefanden pleaded with them not to put him into Midian's bed, and handed over the pact.

As soon as the student had put the pact safely in his pocket he hurried through the gates of hell and back the same way he had come. At the thieves' den he stopped and told old grey-beard about his journey and the kind of bed he had been promised in hell. The old thief now looked frightened and downcast. 'Cheer up!' encouraged the student. 'There is still time to repent and go to heaven.' Old grey-beard, however, shook his head sadly. 'There are too many sins on my conscience for me to win salvation,' he said ruefully. To this the student replied, 'Before I leave you I will plant this oak stick outside your house, and from it you will see whether you may still reach heaven. As surely as the stick bears

leaves tomorrow morning you will find grace with God.'
Having planted the stick, the student was gone.

When the old thief awoke next morning and looked
out of his bedroom window he was truly amazed, for the
stick that the student had given him had changed into a
beautiful oak-tree. At once he tore down his den of
wickedness and built himself a cottage out in the open
fields, far from the dark wood. He repented of his sins
and in his last years he became as God-fearing a man as
ever lived; but he rejoiced most of all when his sons
followed his example, gave up their thieving and led
good, honest lives.

Within a week of setting out the student had returned
to his home. This time his father didn't cry when he saw
him, and since that day Haltefanden, the lame devil,
has kept well away from Hjørring.

FOUR

The Little Nag

Once upon a time there lived a prince who was the King's only son. He was the most beautiful youth imaginable and had, moreover, a good brain and a kind heart. Unfortunately his position, his brains and his beauty made him haughty. Just as he was beautiful himself so everything else had to be beautiful, and the sight of anything ugly made him feel quite ill.

Now it happened one day when he was out hunting with his courtiers that, as they sat down by the roadside eating their lunch, an old man on a miserable horse came riding towards them. Hump-backed, one-eyed and with a crooked neck, the old man wore poor and tattered clothes – not a very beautiful sight, to be sure. Nor was his nag any prettier, for it was a little fat-bellied, long-haired peasant horse with a lame foreleg which made it look uglier still.

'Huh!' shuddered the prince. 'Get rid of that ugly old fellow and his nasty old nag! I can't bear to see anything so frightful.' His courtiers immediately removed the shabby rider from sight.

The old man, however, was not what he seemed to be. He was a great and mighty wizard who did not always appear in such humble guises. Thus, one day when the prince went out alone into the wood the old one-eyed man appeared before him, touched him with his stick and said, 'Now you may see what it's like to be an old nag like mine; and as a horse you shall remain until an innocent princess calls you her very dearest friend.' As he spoke these words the beautiful prince was transformed into an ugly little nag, just like the one his courtiers had chased away.

In the prince's home there was great consternation. The King's son had disappeared, and no one knew his whereabouts.

Meanwhile he was wandering about in the wood in the guise of a small humble peasant nag, very disgruntled and displeased with himself. It was no good returning to his father's palace for he knew that no one there would recognize him. He had been walking about in the woods for two or three days when a small peasant boy happened to come along, gathering firewood. Seeing the little nag grazing, he walked up to it, stroked it and talked to it; and the nag followed him wherever he went. Thus he came home with it to his father who had a small farm-house on the edge of the wood. 'Look, father!' he cried, 'here is a new nag instead of the old one who broke his leg yesterday.' 'That hardly improves matters,' replied his father, looking the animal up and down, 'for this one here seems worn out. It doesn't look worth its keep, but I suppose we'll give it a trial.'

The peasant led the nag to its stable and next day harnessed it to his little plough which, surprisingly, it pulled quite well. 'The nag isn't as bad as it looks, after all,' said the peasant to Hans – that was the boy's name. 'You must feed it well so that we can make good use of it.' Hans liked his little nag very much, and he fed it and brushed it and was very kind to it; but it had to work hard for its keep. When the peasant had sown his seed, he said to Hans, 'Tomorrow I want you to ride the little nag up to town and have two shoes put on it, but no more, mark you, for now I intend to sell it.'

The thought of parting with his little nag saddened Hans, for he had grown very attached to it. When he reached town and had the two shoes put on, there came up to him a one-eyed man who began talking to him, inquiring whether he wanted to sell his horse. 'It will cost two hundred rigsdaler' (two hundred florins), said Hans for a joke. 'That is a lot of money for such a horse,' answered the man, 'but, nevertheless, you shall have it.' 'No,' replied Hans, 'it is more than my life is worth to sell it, for it belongs, not to me, but to my father.' 'Then hurry home and ask him if I may buy it!' commanded the man. Hans, however, had no intention of doing that. He mounted the nag and rode it back home; but he did not tell his father that he had been offered two hundred rigsdaler for it. Shortly afterwards there was a market in town and the peasant said to Hans, 'Now you must spruce up the nag; it is going to market today.' Hans was griefstricken. When he realized that nothing would make his father change his mind, he asked if he might take the nag to market; but his father insisted on going alone. 'All right, if you are determined to sell it you must demand three hundred rigsdaler for it,' said Hans. 'You're mad, boy!' exclaimed his father. 'I know very well what the nag is worth. It won't fetch a hundred rigsdaler.' Hans then told him how he had been offered two hundred rigsdaler. 'You fool!' cried his father, boxing his ears. Then he mounted the nag and rode off to market; but he kept turning over in his mind what Hans had told him, and when anybody asked him how much he wanted for his horse, he answered brightly, 'Three hundred rigsdaler.' The buyers laughed at him and sneered, 'Three hundred rigsdaler for that old nag! It isn't worth a hundred.' Nevertheless, the peasant refused to reduce his price, and towards the end of the day there came up to him an old one-eyed man who did not haggle but gave him three hundred rigsdaler, and in exchange received the nag.

The peasant hurried home, extremely pleased with the good bargain, but Hans wept quietly to himself. Next morning his father called him for breakfast as usual, but there was no reply. Hans had gone. 'He has probably gone out to look for his nag,' suggested the peasant's wife; and with that they ceased to worry.

It was indeed quite true that Hans had gone off to search for his dear nag. In the town he discovered that the man who had bought his horse had travelled to a place many miles away. He was rich, they said, and a nobleman; probably he came from the King's castle.

Hans immediately went on his way. The journey took several days, but at last he reached the palace where he asked to be taken into service as a stable-boy. Feeling sorry for Hans, the head of the King's household at once set him to work; and from stable to stable he went, but there was no sign of his little nag.

One day as he was going about his work as usual, Hans noticed a small sleigh standing in the castle court-yard. Suddenly his face lit up, for the horse harnessed to the sleigh was none other than his own little nag. Hans was so pleased that he left what he was doing and went up to it and stroked it. At that very moment the King's youngest daughter, who was still only a child, came running past. Seeing the nag, she pulled up suddenly. 'I should love to have a little horse like that,' she cried. 'I am sure I could both drive the sleigh and ride it, don't you think so, Hans?' Yes, Hans was sure she could. He knew the horse well, he said, and there never was a more faithful creature. The princess ran straight to her father, the King, and asked him to buy the little horse for her. 'But he is such an ugly little beast,' protested the King. 'There are many beautiful horses in my stables. Now go and choose one of those instead.' The princess had set her heart on having the little nag, however, and she kept on asking her father until at last he agreed, and the horse was hers. 'You must look after this horse really well, Hans,' said the little princess. Nothing pleased Hans more than caring for his dear nag, and he kept his promise so faithfully that it grew more and more beautiful every day. Sometimes the little princess used it to pull the sleigh, sometimes she rode it; and she grew to love it very dearly.

When some time had passed it happened that the King's eldest daughter, for the King had two daughters and no sons, had been out fishing in the pond, and there she had lost a ring her mother had given her. The ring was very valuable and also brought good fortune. Both she and her father grieved over its loss, and the King ordered a thorough search, but no one could find it. At last the King announced that the one who found the princess's ring was to marry her and to receive half his kingdom. There were, of course, many princes, knights and noblemen from the same country and from afar who came and searched; and although several lost their lives in this quest, the ring could not be found.

Meanwhile the younger princess loved her little horse more and more as the days went by. She had it shod with four lovely golden shoes and she often kissed and stroked it.

One day when Hans, the stable-boy, was watering the little horse, he saw a lovely big goldfish in the water. He jumped in and tried to catch it, but it slipped from his grasp. A few days later when he was again watering the little nag, it kicked the self-same goldfish ashore with its hoof. At once he took the fish into the King's kitchens and, of course, everyone had to come down to look at it. When it was cut open, there, inside it, lay the princess's ring. Then the King turned to his eldest daughter and said, 'Well, now you must marry Hans, the stable-boy, for he has found your ring.' The princess agreed to do so and Hans certainly didn't say 'no', but added that really he didn't deserve the honour for discovering the ring; it was the princess's horse which had kicked it ashore with its golden shoe.

When the princess heard this, she ran down into the stables to her little horse, flung her arms around its neck, kissed it and cried, 'No, you are not going to have my sister; she can have Hans, the stable-boy; but you I will keep for ever, for you are my very dearest friend.' As she spoke these words there was no horse any more; instead, in her arms stood a lovely young prince. 'Thank you,' he said, and proceeded to tell her his story, how he had been both punished and rewarded. Then they walked together up to the King, and celebrated their wedding on the same day as Hans, the stable-boy, was married to the elder princess. After the ceremony the handsome prince travelled home with his princess to his father's kingdom where his people rejoiced to see him again. He has now rid himself of his haughtiness and is living in joy and bliss with his very dearest friend. And Hans, the stable-boy, is living happily with the elder princess. He now rules the whole of her father's kingdom as the old King is dead.

FIVE

The Little Black Man

A TAILOR AND a cobbler once happened to be travelling together. On their journey they somehow took the wrong turning and eventually found themselves in a deep wood. They were lost. Path after path they tramped, but each time they had to come back to the same place. After many hours they gave up and decided to rest on a tree-trunk. They were just going to sit down when, in the distance, they saw a dragoon heading towards them. Their faces brightened and their spirits rose. But when they discovered that he, too, was hopelessly lost, their hearts sank again. For a long time the three of them wandered about together, first in one direction, then in another. Round and round they went, always returning to the same spot. In the end, weary and hungry, they gave up all hope of ever finding their way out of the wood and just sat down waiting for death.

Suddenly there was a crackling of twigs and a little black man appeared before them. 'If you will belong to me,' he said, 'I will show you the way.' 'It depends on your terms,' answered the dragoon. 'You'll die soon in any case if you stay here,' went on the little man, 'but now I'm going to take you to a place where you can enjoy yourselves and have all the food and drink you want for a whole year; but when the year is up I shall come and fetch you. 'No!' declared the dragoon, 'whether we die now or in a year's time doesn't make much difference; it comes to the same in the end. Unless you can offer us better terms than that, then we had better call an end to the bargaining.' 'All right,' said the little man, 'I'm only thinking of what would be best for you. Still, nobody likes giving anything away without having something in return, so I'll make you another offer: after you have enjoyed yourselves for a year I'll come back and ask each of you a question, and if you can answer it you will be free to go; but the one who answers wrongly belongs to me.' 'That seems a fair bargain to me,' agreed the dragoon, and got up and shook hands with the little black man. The tailor and the cobbler likewise rose to their feet and put a trembling hand on top. They were so frightened that they wished the ground would swallow them up.

Satisfied with the arrangement, the little black man now led his three companions to an inn on the edge of the wood. Here he paid for their keep for a whole year: they were to have the best rooms and the finest food, and for dinner every night they would each have half a bottle of port on the table. The innkeeper gave his word that he would wait on them hand and foot and that he would consider nothing too good for them, but, of course, for all this he would need to be well paid. The little black man at once pulled out his purse and gave the innkeeper a handful of golden coins with the promise of many more if, after a year, the guests looked fat and well.

For ten months the three companions lived like lords and all were happy. From then onwards as their grand life drew to an end, the tailor and the cobbler grew sad and anxious, for they doubted very much whether they could answer the questions and escape from the clutches

D

. . the goblins and the little black man tucked into their meal.

of the wicked little black man. The dragoon, however, was as carefree as the day is long and every morning he rode out into the fresh air; every evening he returned, contented and happy, while all his friends could do was to sit moping with their miserable faces resting on their hands. In vain the dragoon did his best to persuade them that there was no sense in expecting the worst and looking sullen; they might just as well hope for the best and be gay.

One day, only a fortnight before the end of the year, the dragoon went out for his usual ride. On this occasion he took another path which led him to the other side of the wood. There, standing out from the rest because of its great size and beauty, stood a magnificent tree. 'I will climb to the top of this tree,' thought the dragoon, 'and enjoy the view of the surrounding countryside.' He tied his horse near by and after a long hard climb eventually reached the foliage at the top of the tree. The effort had indeed been worth while, for the sheer beauty and distance he could see made him gasp.

He was sitting there enjoying himself when he happened to look down and was amazed to see a goblin carrying a table which he placed in the shade of his own tree. A few seconds later there came another goblin, this time with three chairs. Then the dragoon's eyes nearly popped out of his head, for who should come next but the little black man, holding a juicy piece of roast beef which he placed on the table. Without further ado, the goblins and the little black man tucked into their meal, smacking their lips and grunting with pleasure. The sight of this food even made the dragoon's mouth water.

It pleased the little black man to see that the others were enjoying themselves. 'Yes, this meat is certainly very tender and tasty, too,' he said; 'but shortly I hope to invite you to an even better meal, for I am fattening up three men in the inn. They have been there for nearly a year now living on the fat of the land. I am sure they will provide the tastiest meat we have ever had.' At this his guests sat up and inquired how he had managed to catch these three men. He told them how they had lost their way and of the bargain he had made with them. He would only free them, he said, if each answered his question correctly, but he was convinced none of them would succeed. 'Listen, and I'll tell you the questions,' he went on. 'In front of the tailor I shall put a lovely piece of material which is really a piece of leather, but not even an expert could tell the difference. I shall give the cobbler something just like a piece of leather but he won't know that it is really a piece of calico. For the dragoon I shall bring a horse more beautiful than he has ever seen before and ask him what is wrong with it. Of course, he won't be able to tell that he is looking at a stag. None of them will be able to tell what I have given them and they will all be mine,' chuckled the little black man, rubbing his hands. In the course of the conversation the meal ended and they parted, looking forward to the next time they would meet.

The dragoon heard every word, and when they had disappeared he hastily climbed down the tree and, very pleased with what he had found out, rode back to the inn. There, as usual, were the tailor and the cobbler, so miserable and crestfallen that they could hardly bother to wish him good evening; whereupon the dragoon went up to them, gave them a good shaking and cried, 'A fat lot of use you've been with all your misery. If you had gone out like me you might have heard or seen something to help us out of our plight.' 'Stop preaching!' they moaned; 'what good has your riding around in the wood done us, eh?' 'You'll understand when you hear what I have to tell you,' replied the dragoon, and he started to tell them what had happened that day. The tailor and the cobbler immediately cocked their ears and listened to every word. When he had finished they kept on asking what answers they should give the little black man, but, much to their annoyance, the dragoon refused to help them. He said the other two didn't deserve to know since they had been so grumpy whereas he had always been gay. He continued to torment them for over an hour, but when he considered they had learnt their lesson, he told each of them what to answer.

Exactly a year to the day after he had left them the little black man made his way to the inn, certain of having one of the three, but hoping for more. He licked his lips, thinking of the fine meal he and his goblin friends would enjoy. As soon as he arrived he went up to the tailor and placed before him a beautiful piece of material and asked him what was wrong with it. The tailor turned it over and said, 'It's certainly very nice, but I think it's a piece of leather you've given me.' This correct answer surprised the little black man, but he consoled himself with the thought that the tailor was a lean man anyhow and there wouldn't be much meat on him. Next came the turn of the cobbler. A piece of lovely leather was placed before him and he was asked to say what was the matter with it. 'This isn't leather at all, but calico!' he cried. The little black man was dumbfounded, but when he had recovered from the shock, he was secretly pleased that the dragoon remained, for he looked the healthiest of them all, since the others were pale and thin from worry. When the dragoon saw the animal, he pretended this was the finest horse he had ever seen and asked if he might have a ride on it. Encouraged by this reply, the little black man agreed, and with a jump the dragoon was on its back and off they went like lightning. He rode all day long and it was not until evening that he returned. He went up to the little black man and cried, 'Do you think I don't know the difference between a horse and a stag when I've been riding horses for years?' The little black man's eyes flashed with anger, and when soon afterwards the innkeeper handed him the bill for keeping the three for a whole year, he threw his bag of coins on the table and stamped off out.

The very next moment the dragoon and his two companions found themselves back in the forest, lost in exactly the same place as before. Again the little black man appeared before them; again he promised to show them out of the forest, but this time they must answer everybody who spoke to them with these words: 'It is right for that money, indeed it is.' This seemed easy enough and so they accepted.

On their way out of the wood they went by the inn where the three had stayed during the past year. They were surprised to hear the sound of shouting and quarrelling, and they decided to call and see what was happening. They soon found out. Apparently during the night a large sum of money had been stolen from a wealthy traveller who was furiously trying to pin the blame on someone. His chance now came. When the three were questioned and all they could answer was, 'It is right for that money, indeed it is,' everyone suspected them and they were immediately taken to court. Each time the judge questioned them, they answered, 'It is right for that money, indeed it is'; whereupon he immediately sentenced them to be hanged as common thieves. Then the judge announced the time and place of the execution.

On the appointed day a great crowd gathered on the top of the hill around the gallows. From miles around whole families, inquisitive and excited, had come to see the hanging. Just before the hangman arrived, the three were given a last chance to prove their innocence, but even then they repeated the words, 'It is right for that money, indeed it is.' Thus, the black cloth was pulled over their faces and the hangman got ready. Just then, however, everyone turned and saw in the distance a coach pulled by four black horses, which galloped towards the hill. As such a fine coach was rarely seen in the neighbourhood and as the nobleman inside might be bringing information about the robbery, they decided to await its arrival before proceeding with the execution. At the foot of the hill the coach stopped and out stepped, not a nobleman as everyone supposed, but a little black man. He ran up the hill to the hangman, tore the black cloth from the dragoon, the tailor and the cobbler, and shouted, 'Let these men go, for they are innocent. The man you are looking for is the innkeeper.' Straightway, the crowd went to the inn and found the stolen money hidden under his bed. The innkeeper now had to confess, and he was hanged at the top of the hill. So the onlookers had their excitement, after all, and went away well satisfied.

The little black man was proud of the three companions for they had shown that they could both speak, and be silent, whenever the need arose; and from then on he allowed them to go wherever they wanted and to say whatever they wished.

SIX

The Twin Brothers

ON A SMALL-HOLDING near the sea there once lived a
childless couple, both getting on in years and very lonely.
They worked hard, struggling to scratch a living from
the barren soil; but so little did they grow that for their
food and keep they depended almost entirely on the
sea, and the man used to go fishing whenever the
weather allowed. In this way they managed to keep
body and soul together for a whole year. But without
warning the weather changed. Storms raged and the
wind blew landwards, making it impossible for anyone
to put to sea. These conditions lasted for several days
until one morning the weather improved and boats
could sail again.

The man now wanted to go to sea, but his wife didn't
favour the idea for it was Whitsun, and she warned him
that no luck would come to anyone who went fishing,
or who did any other work on such a Holy Day; but
they were so poor and it was so long since they had
tasted any real food that the husband felt he had to seize
this opportunity, and taking his net, float and line, he
quickly rowed out to sea.

Whenever he fished, however, he failed to catch anything until late in the day he pulled out a single fish – a
weird, big ugly one unlike any he had ever seen before.
Believing it to be of no use, he threw it back in the

water and went on fishing. Again he had no luck until some time afterwards he drew out the self-same fish for the second time; and immediately he threw it back again. He was determined not to return empty-handed and continued fishing, but all he managed to catch was the ugly fish for the third time. He hauled it inside the boat and took it off the hook, intending to throw it back into the sea once more. At the same time he decided he had done enough fishing for one day. His wife had probably been right; it *was* unlucky to fish on a Holy Day. That very moment, however, the fish began to talk. 'Please don't despise me. I'm a better catch than you imagine,' it said; 'take me home and you will not regret it.' 'What good will that do me?' asked the man. 'Listen carefully to everything I say,' went on the fish. 'As soon as you get home cut me open, take out all my insides and throw them on the manure heap. Then scrape all the scales off me, making sure none are lost. Next, you must cut off my head and bury it underneath a stone near your house. The shoulder-piece you must boil and give your wife to eat, but remember not to have any of it yourself. She will then bear you two sons.

'The rest of my body must be preserved very carefully until your boys are seven years old. On their seventh birthday cut it up into three parts. Give the stomach-piece to your young mare, the second piece to your bitch and the tail you must tie to a branch in the tall tree near your small-holding where the hawk builds its nest. Your mare will then have two foals, your dog two puppies and the hawk two fledglings. All these you must keep and rear. Now when the boys reach the age of fifteen, dig down by the stone where you laid my head. You will find the jaw-bones have been changed into two swords and my ear-bones will have become two knives. Give each of your sons a sword and a knife, and one of the horses, dogs and hawks which you have reared. The scales that you have kept will by then have turned into golden coins and these you must share equally between the two boys: they will then be well provided for. The animals, too, will be very useful to them and the sword is so made that everything they strike at must fall; and from the knives it can be seen whether danger threatens your sons, for if this should be, they will quickly rust. From that day onwards you and your wife will want for nothing and you need never go to sea again. Your soil will grow good crops and your animals will do well. You will become prosperous and you will be able to give your sons a good start in life. Remember carefully all I have said and follow my instructions closely, otherwise some misfortune will befall you.'

The fish said no more and died that very instant. Hurriedly the man turned his boat towards the shore and made for home. As soon as he reached his small-holding he did everything the fish had told him. He cut it open, threw its insides on the manure heap, scraped off all the scales and put them in safe keeping; then he cut off the head and buried it under a stone. Finally he boiled the shoulder-piece and gave it his wife to eat; the rest of the fish he kept in brine.

Nine months later his wife gave birth to two boys who grew up into bonny children, as clever and as handsome as could be. Their long hair shone like gold and they were as alike as two drops of water. Whether at work or play they remained always together, and so much did they love each other that never a cross word passed between them.

On their seventh birthday the old man remembered to do as the fish had said and got hold of its body, cutting it into three pieces. He gave the stomach-piece to his young mare, the next to his yellow bitch and the tail he hung up outside his small-holding in a tall tree where the hawk had built its nest. Immediately the mother bird caught hold of it and took it to its nest. The black mare foaled at the appointed time and had two lovely colts, while the yellow bitch gave birth to two beautiful little puppies; and soon afterwards there appeared in the nest two young hawks which the man caught and tamed. Of the two foals, the two puppies and the two hawks, each pair was identical so that the one could not be told from the other. When the boys were fifteen, the old man went to the stone and dug under it. Here, as the fish had foretold, he found two shining swords and two sharp knives; and when he went to look at the scales he found hundreds of bright golden coins. The man divided the money equally between his two sons and gave each of them a sword and a knife, telling them the qualities the weapons possessed. Then he gave each a horse, a dog and a hawk which resembled each other as closely as did the two brothers themselves. Finally they received reins, saddles and fine clothes, all alike. 'Now,' said the father, 'you are both of age and you are your own masters. You may do whatever you wish. Either you may stay at home or you may go out into the world and seek your fortune.'

Eager for adventure, the two brothers decided to go at once into the wide world. They tied their swords at their hips and put their knives in their belts. Then they said good-bye to their parents, and with their hair shining like gold they jumped on to their magnificent black stallions. Each had a hawk on his shoulder and their dogs bounded ahead of them. They travelled together for many days, riding along the dark forest paths. People they met by the wayside stood still and stared at the two brothers, for they were so handsome and alike.

On and on they travelled, but never an opportunity arose for them to prove their courage and their strength. Thus one day when they arrived at a clearing in the wood where the paths divided, they agreed to go separate ways. Before parting, however, they drew their knives and stuck them into a lime-tree. Each then promised to return once every year to see whether the other's knife was bright or rusty; if the latter, the one would know that his brother was in mortal danger. And so they said good-bye, the elder twin – he who came first into the world – taking the path to the right, the younger the one to the left.

The elder brother rode from one town to another, from one county to the next until late one evening he reached the King's city and pulled up at an inn which stood opposite the royal palace. Now, when early the next morning he unfastened the shutters and looked out of the window, he saw that the palace was draped in black from top to bottom. He called the innkeeper and asked him what was the matter.

'You must have come a long way, young sir, not to know what great trouble has befallen us. The King has had to promise his only daughter, who is barely sixteen years old and very beautiful, to a gruesome merman since otherwise this fiend will lay our country waste; and it is this very day, in an hour's time, that the merman must have her. That is why the whole town is in mourning. The King has announced that anyone who saves his daughter from the merman may marry her and inherit the kingdom after his death, and a knight by name of Ridder Rød has volunteered to protect her, saying that if he fails he will take his own life. But nobody has any faith in him; so unless a miracle happens we shall lose our princess.'

An hour later there came out of the palace gates a

closed carriage pulled by six black horses and draped in black, as were the coachman and all the servants. The coach, with the princess dressed all in white sitting inside, turned slowly towards the sea-shore. Behind rode Ridder Rød in full harness with helmet and shield, sword and lance. The people who lined the streets wept and wailed as the princess drove past.

Through the wood, down to the sea-shore rolled the carriage. Here where the trees grew right up to the water's edge was the place chosen by the merman. As soon as the princess had descended from the coach, the driver and servants rode off as fast as they could, for they were terrified in case the merman came after them. When they had gone, Ridder Rød, as frightened as a rabbit, also hurried into the wood. He tied his horse to a tree and climbed up into the high branches. After the merman had taken the princess, he thought, he would ride home and tell how bravely he had defended her; as no one was present to contradict him, he hoped that, for his courage, he would rise in the estimation of the King and might even inherit the kingdom after his death.

The elder brother saw from his window the princess leaving the palace, and shortly afterwards he mounted his black stallion and rode off with his hawk, his dog and his shining sword. Soon he was galloping towards the sea-shore where the princess sat alone in the shade of a tree awaiting the merman. He jumped from his horse, greeted her and asked why she was crying. She told him all and added, 'Ridder Rød promised to save me, but now he has gone away. There is the merman,' she screamed suddenly, and at the same moment she fainted. From out of the sea came a roar, and a huge black wave, edged with white foam, rolled shorewards. In it was the merman who had no less than nine heads which all bellowed at the same time, 'Who is with my betrothed?'

'She's not yours, but mine,' answered the elder brother, jumping into his saddle. 'We will fight to decide that,' challenged the merman. 'All right, we'll fight,' agreed the youth. Thus saying, he drew his sword and shouted, 'Hawk, hound, and horse, attack!' They made straight for the merman and clashed at the water's edge. The hawk pecked the merman's eyes, the dog seized his necks, the horse bit and kicked while the brother swung his sword, chopping off three of the merman's heads; these the dog dragged ashore.

Exhausted, the merman gasped, 'Wait until tomorrow. I'm going now to gather my strength.' Back with his six heads he went into the depths of the sea, leaving behind him a trail of red blood on the foam. The brother wrenched open the mouths of the three heads, cut out the tongues, wrapped them in the princess's handkerchief and stored them safely. Then, after

They made straight for the merman a

wiping his sword on the grass, he rode off with his hawk and his dog to the inn.

Ridder Rød, who sat trembling in the tree, had seen the merman arrive, but could not see where the struggle took place. All he heard was a roaring and a screaming and the sounds of battle. The parting words of the merman also reached his ears: 'Tomorrow at the same time.' Then he saw the merman returning to sea again with the red foam rising above him.

The knight hurried down the tree and along the shore to the princess. Seeing she had fainted, he dashed seawater in her face to revive her, and when she opened

shed at the water's edge

her eyes he told her how he had fought the merman and chopped off three of his heads; but the princess who had seen part of the struggle refused to believe him. 'Unless you swear to tell everyone it was I who fought the merman, I'll slay you this very moment,' he cried angrily. Reluctantly, the frightened princess promised to do as he said.

After lifting the princess on to his saddle, Ridder Rød tied one head to the horse's tail and the other two to its mane, and thus he rode up to the city and through the streets which were thronged with people, wild with joy. 'Hurrah for the princess and hurrah for Ridder Rød!' everyone shouted, and followed them to the palace where the King received them. There, Ridder Rød told in great detail of his battle with the merman, pointing to the three heads he had chopped off. 'The merman is coming back tomorrow,' warned the knight, 'and the princess must meet him at the same place. But never fear, I shall be there to save her.' Afraid to contradict him because of her promise, the princess remained silent except to say, as was true, that she had fainted while the fight took place.

Now Ridder Rød thought that the stranger who had so bravely fought the merman that day would probably lose his life during the next encounter. If the merman were killed, it would be so much the better, for then he was certain to win the princess and inherit the kingdom. Should the merman be the victor and take the princess with him, however, he would still be rewarded for his gallantry.

Early the following morning, again dressed in white, the princess set off to meet the merman, but this time she rode in a silver carriage and the six horses which pulled it were grey. Behind rode Ridder Rød in full harness, with his helmet and shield, his sword and his lance. This time the onlookers were no longer sad for they had faith in the brave knight. 'Hurrah for the princess! Hurrah for Ridder Rød!' they shouted.

They reached the appointed place and the princess stepped down from the coach which then hurried off to a clearing deep in the forest where it was to wait until the fight was over. As soon as it was out of sight Ridder Rød bade the princess good-bye and rode off to his hiding-place. Here he tethered his horse and climbed up into the foliage.

Meanwhile, at the inn, the elder brother had seen the coach drive off. He at once mounted his horse and galloped towards the beach. There he found the princess both relieved and happy to see him, but in her heart she felt ashamed for having allowed Ridder Rød to receive all the praise. No sooner had they spoken, however, than they heard a terrible roar, and turning, saw a huge black wave, edged with white foam, rolling towards them. From many throats they heard a strange voice, shouting, 'Who is there with my betrothed?' It was the merman. The brother saw that he had grown three new heads in place of those he had lost yesterday, and he seemed as strong as ever.

Unafraid, he answered, 'She is not yours, but mine.' 'We'll fight to decide that,' roared the merman. 'Yes, we'll fight,' replied the youth, springing into his saddle. He quickly drew his sword and shouted, 'Hawk, hound and horse, attack!' They all dashed straight for the merman and came to grips at the water's edge. The battle raged long and furiously with the hawk pecking, the dog biting and the horse kicking. Blow after blow the youth struck with his sword until six of the merman's nine heads rolled off into the sea; and one by one the dog brought them back to the shore.

The merman was now so weak that he decided to call

E

a halt to the battle for that day. 'Wait until tomorrow,' he gasped; 'I'm going to regain my strength.' And surrounded by blood-red foam, he retreated into the depths.

The youth then cut out the tongues of the six heads and added them to the three he had already wrapped in the princess's handkerchief. He wiped his red sword on the green grass, whistled his hawk and his dog and walked slowly towards his horse. Now this time the princess had not fainted but had watched every second of the terrible struggle. She now ran up to the elder brother, flung her arms around his neck and kissed him. Tears rolled down her cheeks as she thanked him for saving her. The youth kissed her in return; then, mounting his black stallion, he soon disappeared into the forest.

From his hiding-place, all Ridder Rød saw was the merman retreating to his home, and all he heard was his promise to continue the battle on the following day. He was soon at the princess's side and, pointing a knife at her heart, he forced her to promise to tell everyone that he had saved her yet again. He collected the six heads of the merman, fetched the silver carriage, and with the princess inside, drove off towards town.

In front of the coach hung the six heads of the merman, and Ridder Rød acknowledged the cheers of the crowds who followed him and the princess to the palace gates. Here the King greeted them, kissed his daughter and wept for joy. Although Ridder Rød let it be known that the battle would be renewed on the morrow, everyone was convinced that on the third and last day he would destroy the merman, take the princess for his bride and inherit the kingdom. The black cloth was at once removed from every building, and feasting and merrymaking went on until the late hours.

At sunrise, the princess, still in white, rode off towards the sea-shore; but this time the coach was golden and the horses were draped in scarlet; and the riders, coach-man and servants who accompanied her were all clad in red livery with gold tresses front and back. Behind came Ridder Rød; and to waving and cheering the procession made its way to the beach.

As on the previous two occasions the princess climbed down from the coach on the sea-shore, and the coach-man with the servants and six riders drove off into the wood. When they were out of sight Ridder Rød said good-bye to the princess and returned to his hiding-place in the tree. There he watched and waited. Now as he sat there Ridder Rød made his plans. If the stranger slew the merman and claimed the princess as his bride, no one would believe him, for had not the princess supported Ridder Rød's story on the first two occasions? On the other hand, if the merman were victorious and killed both the stranger and the princess, only he could tell what happened, and thus he would become successor to the King.

For this, their third encounter, the merman arrived earlier than usual, and with a great roar the giant wave rolled towards the shore. He now had all his nine heads again and, stronger than ever, he was determined to get his revenge.

Meanwhile the brother, galloping down to the shore, saw the merman emerge from the water and advance towards the princess. 'Faster, faster!' he called to his horse, and on they sped. There was no time even to wave to the princess. He reached the beach, jumped from his horse and immediately joined battle. The struggle raged for most of the morning until at last the nine heads of the merman lay scattered on sea and sand. Weary and wounded, the elder brother staggered ashore. He reached the edge of the wood and then collapsed, falling into a deep slumber; and while he slept the princess watched over him, stroking his forehead and tending his wounds. Now the battle had ended the black horse grazed peacefully and the hawk slept on a branch overhanging its master; but the dog ran off into the wood and finally lay down on the soft moss under the tree occupied by Ridder Rød.

The knight had watched the merman coming out of the dark wave and had heard him roaring and shrieking as he lost his heads; suddenly silence had fallen, and seeing no merman return to the sea, he sat tense and anxious, wondering what had happened. At last he could wait no longer and decided to climb down the tree. Just then, however, he heard a rustling of leaves near by; and when he saw the big yellow dog, he thought it was one of the merman's sea-hounds and he kept deathly still, his forehead glistening with sweat.

Meanwhile the elder brother slept deeply and the princess sat beside him. She took his golden ring from his finger and tied it to his golden hair. When in the late afternoon he eventually awoke, she asked him to take her home to her father's palace and receive the honour due to him. Then together, she thought, they would expose the lies of Ridder Rød. The elder brother, however, had to refuse, for many months had passed since he and his brother had parted, and he must hurry to the lime-tree in the forest far away; but he vowed to return a year from that very day and make the princess his bride. He returned to the water's edge and cut out the tongues of the merman, storing them with the others in the princess's handkerchief. Then he whistled his hawk and his dog, jumped on to his horse and rode off.

When the dog had gone Ridder Rød uttered a deep sigh of relief, climbed down the tree and crept towards the edge of the wood from where he could see the beach. There lay the merman, all his heads, arms and legs severed from his body. Then he saw the princess, alone and sad. Up to her he went, threatening to kill her unless she told everyone that he had slain the merman. Too frightened to disobey, she made her promise, hoping that her hero would return to rescue her in a year's time. Gloating over his good fortune, Ridder Rød fetched the golden carriage, collected the merman's heads and hung them around the coach, and with the princess beside him he proudly rode up to the city. There, the crowds had grown anxious, for many hours had passed since the princess had set off for the seashore. Suddenly the rumbling of the carriage and the galloping of the horses could be heard, and a few seconds later all could see that the princess had been saved by the gallant knight. 'Hurrah for the princess, hurrah for Ridder Rød!' they shouted, as the procession went by.

At the palace Ridder Rød told his story to the King, and the same day he was betrothed to the princess and appointed heir to the kingdom. Toasts were drunk and bonfires blazed all over the land. Although the princess agreed to the wedding, she insisted on waiting a year, and as the King approved of this arrangement, there was little Ridder Rød could do about it.

Far from the scene of his triumph, the elder brother, Troldbane ('Killer of the Merman'), was riding furiously with his hawk and his dog towards the crossroads where a year ago he had said good-bye to his brother. He reached the forest clearing, peered in the direction of the lime-tree and saw that neither knife was tarnished; but from the sign cut deeply in the bark he knew that his brother had recently been there and decided to follow his path. From town to town he travelled, but wherever he inquired no one had news of the younger brother. On and on he went and the months slipped by. At last he realized that if he were to keep his promise to the beautiful princess he would have to give up the search. Thus, with his hawk and his dog, he galloped swiftly towards the King's city which he left nearly a year ago.

As he entered the town Troldbane was surprised to see flags flying and all the houses garlanded. The inn was decorated and the palace was covered with scarlet. At the inn he left his horse, hawk and dog in the stables and was given the same room as the one he occupied a year ago. He called the innkeeper and said, 'Whenever I am in your town there is always something important happening. Last year you were in mourning because of the merman. Now this year the flags are flying and everywhere is decorated with flowers. What is it this time?' The innkeeper told him that today they were celebrating the wedding of the princess to Ridder Rød. 'We must drink their health,' said Troldbane. 'Fetch a bottle of wine.' His host fetched a bottle and poured wine for both. 'This wine doesn't agree with me!' exclaimed the elder brother, lowering his glass; 'I'm sure that on the King's table the wine tastes much better.' 'I'm certain of that,' agreed the innkeeper, sighing, 'I wish we had some of it.' 'I'll soon get some for us,' said Troldbane, and whistled his hawk. When the bird had settled on his shoulder he whispered something to it, and in a flash it had disappeared through the window in the direction of the palace.

Meanwhile in the long banqueting hall everyone sat ready to begin the feast. Suddenly a flapping of wings caused the guests to look up; there above them hovered the hawk, which finally swooped and settled on the princess's right shoulder. She at once recognized it and stroked it lovingly. But the bird did not stay long. It snatched at the decanter on the royal table and, before anyone realized what was happening, it had flown off the way it had come. Only a few seconds later the hawk placed the wine before its master who poured his host and himself a full glass and proposed a toast to the princess and her future husband. The wine was so beautiful that the innkeeper became dizzy and said, 'I only wish we had some of the King's cakes and biscuits, too; they would go well with this wine.' 'Then we shall have some,' replied the elder brother who straightway whistled his dog. Up the stairs came his hound and stood at its master's side. Troldbane whispered a few words in its ear and off it bounded towards the palace, and hard as the sentries and servants tried, they could not prevent the dog from crossing the palace courtyard and entering the great banqueting hall. The guests had only just settled down after the previous disturbance when there was a scuffle in the corridor, the door burst open and in raced the hound. Straight for the royal table it ran and buried its head in the princess's lap. Ridder Rød jumped up as though he had seen the Devil. 'That is the merman's sea-hound!' he exclaimed, terrified. 'That's no sea-hound,' she replied, 'it's a good Danish dog, and surely you can't be afraid of a sea-hound after having fought the merman with nine heads.' The guests all laughed at this, but Ridder Rød kept eyeing the big yellow dog suspiciously, for he well remembered how it had rested under his tree after the final battle on the beach. Suddenly the dog sprang on to the table, grabbed the silver basket of cakes and biscuits, and out of the room it dashed, down the corridor, across the courtyard past the startled sentries and over to the inn.

Meanwhile in the banqueting hall confusion reigned,

... there hovered the hawk which finally swooped

but the princess was secretly happy and excited for she was convinced that her true betrothed was near at hand. Now it was the custom in those days that after the feast and before the actual wedding, all the King's subjects visited the palace to wish the bride and bridegroom well. Among those who came were Troldbane and the innkeeper. In one of the crowded halls the elder brother suddenly stopped, for along the walls stood nine lances, and on top of each lance was a merman's head. He went up to each lance in turn and forced open each mouth, demanding, 'Where is the tongue?' All eyes turned towards the handsome stranger and everyone began to take notice. Then they looked at Ridder Rød, expecting him to satisfy the stranger's curiosity. The deceitful knight came up to Troldbane, saying, 'The merman had no tongues.' Looking into one of the

nd settled on the princess's right shoulder

mouths again, Troldbane answered, 'That's very strange
for the roots are still here,' and untying the princess's
handkerchief he revealed the nine tongues, each of
which fitted exactly into the merman's heads. 'Now you
may judge for yourselves,' he announced, 'whether the
one who cut out the tongues killed the merman or
whether it was he who chopped off the heads and said
there were no tongues.'

Immediately there was great excitement. Everyone
looked at the heads and saw that the tongues fitted, and
the princess, unable to contain herself any longer, ran
up to Troldbane, flung her arms around his neck and
cried, 'This is the man who fought the merman three
times to save me.' She told how each time Ridder Rød
had left her before the arrival of the merman, and how
each time he had returned when the battle was over.

Then she pointed to the handkerchief in which Troldbane had wrapped the merman's tongues, and everyone, seeing her name and crown upon it, knew that it
was hers. 'When this man slept after the third battle,'
she continued, looking at Troldbane, 'I took the golden
ring from his finger and tied it in his hair.' With these
words she untied the ring from his hair and showed it to
the King.

Faced with all this evidence, Ridder Rød admitted
everything the princess had said. The King immediately
ordered his servants to put him in chains and to take
him to the tree which had been his hide-out during the
elder brother's battles with the merman. Here he was
hanged and soon forgotten.

The wedding between the princess and Troldbane
was celebrated that same night, and the old King, who
had reigned for many years, decided to give up his
throne in favour of his son-in-law. When the celebrations had ended, the King and his Queen journeyed to
the four corners of the kingdom to enable their subjects
to pay homage.

Now it happened that on the first night after his return to his capital, Troldbane noticed a cock sitting
outside the window. The bird crowed and crowed until
the young King, tired of the noise, chased it away; but
no matter how often he frightened the bird off, it always
came back, perched itself on the window-sill and went
on crowing. Neither the King nor his wife got a wink of
sleep. By the next night the King had forgotten about
the bird and both he and his wife went to bed as usual.
No sooner had they fallen asleep, however, than the
shrill crowing of the cock startled them. Thus they
passed a second sleepless night. When on the third night
the bird came again, crowing more loudly than ever,
the young King could stand no more. 'This is no ordin-

ary bird,' he said; 'it probably means that some misfortune has befallen my brother. I must hasten to find out.'

He said good-bye to his wife and begged her not to worry; and having girded on his sword and summoned his horse, hawk and dog, he was soon riding across the cobbled courtyard, through the gates and out into the darkness. Ahead of him crowed the cock, guiding him on through the forest, down to the sea-shore and near the scene of his struggle with the merman. But so thick was the fog that he did not know whether he was on sea or land.

Suddenly Troldbane realized that he could no longer hear the crowing of the bird and brought his horse to a halt. For a while he sat still in the saddle, listening intently for the cock. Not a sound could be heard, however, and he had just decided to return to the palace when he heard a noise near by. There, coming towards him carrying a sack, was an old hag using her stick to guide her. 'Who are you and what brings you here so early in the morning?' demanded the King. 'Good sir, I am only a poor childless woman. I gather bones, but as you can see it is all I can do to keep myself upright, let alone my sack. If you are a kind man you will let your horse carry my sack home for me.' 'Where do you live?' asked the King. 'Not far away,' the old woman replied. 'If you will take my sack I will walk ahead and you can follow me.' The King quickly dismounted and flung the sack across the horse's back. Into the sea went the hag, hitting the water with her stick and murmuring, 'Bridge in front and bridge behind,' and immediately dry land appeared wherever they walked. But on all sides lay the deep sea and the thick fog. Close behind her, not knowing the way, followed the King with his

At this the hag suddenly straightened up . . .

horse, his hawk and his dog. The journey seemed endless and at last the King said, 'It's a long way to your home.' 'We shall soon be there,' answered the old hag. Finally they came to a high mountain in the middle of the sea. The woman tapped a rock with her stick and there opened in front of them a big room with high stone walls, and in the middle of the floor blazed a roaring fire. The King lifted down the heavy sack containing the smelly bones and exclaimed jokingly, 'What a good fire you have! I suppose you roast men on it, don't you?' 'Oh, no!' she replied, 'when you are as old as I am you must have warmth.' Then she pulled a hair from her head and bade the King put it on his horse to make it stand still, otherwise, she said, it might stamp through the floor. The King obeyed, but he didn't hear the old hag murmur, 'Hairs turn into iron chains and hold fast.' At once the horse stood as still as a statue. She then plucked another hair from her head and said to the King, 'Go and put this hair on the dog for he looks so wickedly at me!' Again the King obeyed, and again after she had murmured her words the dog, too, stood quite still. For the third time she pulled out a hair and asked the King to throw it on the hawk since she thought the bird would frighten her chicks. Thinking this request reasonable, the King did as she said. Again, unheard by the King, the old hag murmured her magic words and the hawk sat motionless. Then she said, 'I wish you would throw a hair on your sword; it is so bright that it dazzles my poor old eyes.' Once more the King did as she asked while she whispered the self-same words.

Although he thought the old woman was mad, the King was not afraid of her and asked if he might look around her house. At this the hag suddenly straightened up until she was as tall as the ceiling, and with an evil look on her face, she screamed, 'Now I'll pay you back for killing my dear son! Every night I go out to gather his bones on the sea-shore, and when I have collected them all I shall try to bring him back to life again.' The King now realized whose house he had visited and straightway uttered his war cry, 'Horse, hawk and hound, attack!' But the witch laughed and said, 'No, they can't move for my hairs have become chains.' Troldbane then reached for his sword, but he was unable to move it. Suddenly, with her stick the wicked witch struck him such a mighty blow that the young King fell to the floor, dead, and she kicked him down into her cellar, leaving his animals as they were.

Meanwhile in the palace the young Queen wondered what had happened to her husband. She sat by her window for hours at a time, but there was no sign of him. Weeks passed, then months. To every part of the kingdom riders were sent to search for him, but never could they find anyone who had seen him. In her heart, however, the Queen believed that one day her hero would come home again.

Now it happened that the younger of the twins had travelled far and wide in many lands. Difficulties and dangers he had encountered, but he had always emerged from them successfully. He was now riding back to the lime-tree for it was a year since his last visit, when all had been well. Then, his brother's knife had shone brightly but now, as he pulled it from the trunk, he saw that it was rusty to the hilt and was stained with blood.

Then he turned down the path his brother had first taken and galloped off. From town to town he sped, day after day, night after night, until at long last as dusk was falling he reached the capital of his brother's country. As he rode, with his hawk on his shoulder and his dog bounding beside him, he noticed that everyone greeted him, waving happily. From this he gathered that his brother, for whom he was mistaken since he resembled him so closely, was very popular and highly thought of. He acknowledged the cheers and rode on to the palace where, to his great surprise, the sentries jumped to attention and presented arms. Evidently this was his brother's home, for all the ostlers and servants ran to the gates, delighted to see him. His horse was taken to the stables, and into the palace he went. There he was welcomed by the beautiful Queen who flung her arms around his neck and sobbed for joy.

She asked where he had been since that night, three months ago, when he had followed that cock, whether it carried a message as he had thought, and whether his brother was safe and sound. Still more questions she put to him, stroking the feathers of the hawk, patting the dog and asking how his horse was, for, she said, after him she loved his animals most of all since they had helped to save her from the merman.

The young brother got to know as much as he could without divulging his secret, but at last he begged to be allowed to sleep, promising to answer all her questions on the morrow. He ate his supper and retired to the bedroom. Before undressing, however, he pulled out his sword and placed it in the middle of the bed, pretending to fall asleep from weariness. The Queen lay down, but she was so excited she could not sleep. She thanked God for guarding her husband and bringing him home to her. She looked forward to the next day when the King would tell her of his adventures.

But some time later, the princess heard the crowing of the same cock which had lured her husband away from her a few months ago. Now, she thought, her husband slept too soundly to hear the bird. The younger brother, however, was wide awake, and on hearing the cock, flung aside his bedclothes and buckled his sword. 'You're not going after that cock, again,' she protested, 'for it told you all it knew last time.' But the brother told her that, for a reason he could not now reveal, he was obliged to pursue the bird. He would be back soon and, meanwhile, she was not to worry about him. Out of the door, down the stairs, across the courtyard he dashed, and with his hawk and his dog, he dug his spurs into the black stallion and rode off into the night. Like his brother, the cock led him down to the sea-shore; like his brother he met the old hag with her stick and her sack, gathering bones on the beach in the early morning light. He, too, carried her sack and followed her out into the sea to her mountain home where the big fire blazed. 'Do you roast men on it?' he asked. 'Oh, no!' replied the old hag, 'an old one like me must have warmth.' Then she plucked hairs from her head and, for the same reasons as she had given his brother, asked him to put them on his horse, his dog, his hawk and his sword; but, without her noticing, he threw them into the fire. With a hideous grin on her ugly face, the hag straightened up to the height of the ceiling, and towering above the youth, cried, 'Now I have you in my power, too, and you shall join your brother who slew my dear son.'

At these words the young brother drew his sword, shouting, 'Horse, hawk and hound, attack!' 'They cannot move for the hairs have turned into chains,' leered the witch. But the horse, hawk and the dog were already upon her and their master was swinging his wonderful sword. The old hag realized that she would be overwhelmed and knelt at his feet, begging for mercy. 'Only if you return my twin brother to me alive and well,' said the youth.

In terror of her life, she dragged the King from the cellar, sprinkled drops of life-water on his face and brought him back to life again. The two brothers greeted each other briefly. Then the younger twin forced the old witch to free the King's animals which stood rooted to the floor. 'Now lead us across the sea,' he ordered, and they followed her closely out of her mountain home. 'Bridge in front, bridge behind,' she murmured, and the brothers with their animals rode behind. At long last they reached the shore where, without further ado, the younger brother chopped off her head and left her to lie at the water's edge as food for the wild animals and birds.

Without a glance behind them the two brothers rode off into the forest where they talked about the experiences they had had since they parted by the lime-tree two years ago. When it came to the end of the younger brother's story, he told how he had been mistaken for the King and how at the palace he had rested in the bed next to the Queen. At this the King became so furious that he drew his sword and plunged it into his brother's heart; and the younger brother fell from his horse to the ground, dead. Then, like a madman, the King dug his spurs into his horse and galloped madly into the night, he knew not where. Mile after mile he travelled with his hawk on his shoulder and his dog trailing breathlessly behind. Suddenly the hawk began to speak. 'Ride home, ride home!' it said; at this the King gave the horse its head and it was not long before he reached the palace. He left his horse to a servant and walked slowly up the stairs to his wife. The Queen was happy to see him again, but he avoided both her look and her questions. She saw at once that something was wrong: either

F

there had been an accident or he was ill. Then, without a word, the King flung himself on to the bed. At once the Queen spoke: 'There is one thing you must tell me. Why did you leave your drawn sword in the middle of the bed last night? Did you intend to murder me? If so I wish you had, for then I would not have had to see you in such a rage.'

Slowly it dawned on the King how faithful and true his brother had been. Filled with remorse, he tried to sleep, but his troubled conscience would not let him rest. He rose suddenly, dashed down to the stables and, with his hawk and his dog, rode out into the forest to the spot where he had committed his gruesome deed. There in a pool of blood lay his brother. Overcome with grief, the King jumped off his horse and threw himself over the dead body and sobbed. He could not live on, haunted by his misdeed and without his brother; so, rising to his feet, he drew his sword, intending to kill himself. But at that very moment the flapping of wings startled him, and his brother's hawk, a bottle in its beak, settled on its master's shoulder. He at once recognized the bottle as the one the witch had used and, snatching it from the bird, he poured the life-water over his brother. The younger twin immediately got up, strong and well once more.

The King embraced his brother and begged forgiveness for his hasty action and lack of faith. Then, together, the two brothers rode back to the palace where they told the Queen their story. This made her so happy that she asked Troldbane to share the kingdom with his brother so that they could always be near each other, and to that the King at once agreed. Not many months afterwards the younger brother married a princess from a neighbouring country, and there came to the wedding their aged parents who lived with them the rest of their days. The two brothers, who were now Kings, always agreed and ruled the country firmly but well. And the two Queens and all their children became the closest of friends.

SEVEN

The Boy and the Monk

ONCE UPON A time there was a poor boy who had been in service for three years; and for every year he was paid a penny. He decided that now it was time he had a change, and with three pennies in his pocket he said good-bye to his master and set off on the road. Merrily he skipped along, as happy as a lark and as free as a bird on the wing.

He had not gone far when an old woman came up to him and asked why he danced along the road so light-heartedly. 'I've just finished three years' service,' he replied, 'and for each year I've been paid a penny; so now I'm both rich and happy.' 'Would you give me one of your pennies?' inquired the old woman. 'Yes,' replied the boy unhesitatingly, 'for I shall still have two left.' But the old woman said, 'Would you give me another penny?' 'Yes,' answered the boy, 'for I shall still have one left.' 'Would you give me all three pennies?' asked the old woman. 'All right,' sighed the boy. 'You may as well have them all. I've only got to go into service again for three more years and I shall earn three more pennies.' Thus consoled, he gave her his three pennies, and danced as happily as before. 'As you have been so kind-hearted to me,' interrupted the old woman, 'I will give you three wishes before we part.' The boy's face lit up. 'Let me have a bow and arrows which will hit

everything I aim at. Let me have a fiddle with such a
tune that everybody who hears it must dance and
finally, grant me the wish that anything I ask of either
man or woman may be given to me.' The old woman
immediately gave him a bow and arrows and a fiddle
and promised that all his requests would be fulfilled.

The boy was now very happy and he danced and
skipped along the highway. On the road he met a monk
who went up to him and asked, 'What is it that makes
you so happy and joyful, my boy?' 'Oh! I can shoot a
falcon and I can shoot a hawk,' answered the boy.
'That's why I'm so happy and joyful.' And he danced
on along the road.

The monk decided to accompany the boy and they
went on together until they came to a river. As they
walked along the bank the monk noticed on the far
shore a thorny bush, on top of which was perched a
raven. Then he swore by his mantle so grey that if the
boy could shoot the raven he would swim across and
fetch it. The boy at once took aim and the bird was
shot: and the monk had to swim across the river to
fetch it. Dripping wet and gasping for breath, the monk
finally struggled across to the opposite shore. He had
just reached into the thorny bush to retrieve the raven
when the boy started playing his fiddle. And, however
reluctant he was, the monk had to dance to the music.
'Please stop playing,' he begged. 'Then you may have
all the money lying in my mantle – and there's every bit
of 18,000 kroner which I stole from a house where the
husband was out.' But the boy didn't trust him and
played on. At last, when he felt he could dance no
longer, the monk swore by his mantle so grey that he
would give the boy all his money if only he would stop
playing. The boy now humoured him and the music
stopped; and the monk tore himself away from the

thorny bush. But when he was free the monk regretted his promise. 'If only I hadn't sworn by my mantle so grey,' he thought, 'I wouldn't give the boy so much as a penny.'

The boy and the monk walked on together until they came to a big town. Here the angry monk went up to the authorities and accused the boy of having stolen the 18,000 kroner that had been in his mantle. Of course, they found the money on the boy and he was sentenced to be hanged. The rope was already in place around his neck when he asked if he might have his fiddle; and as neither man nor woman could refuse him whatever he requested, the executioner jumped down from the scaffold and fetched it for him. Meanwhile, the monk, seeing the fiddle being taken to the boy, demanded to be tied to a tree.

As soon as the boy started playing his fiddle, the executioner jumped down and began dancing. He was joined by the authorities who danced and hopped until they were almost exhausted. As for the monk, who had been tied to a tree, he stamped and stumped and jigged and jumped.

Presently the authorities appealed to the boy to stop playing and promised to spare his life if he would do so. He stopped at once, and when they were still, he told them how things had happened from first to last between the monk and himself. The monk was hanged in his place and the boy travelled on with his fiddle. He still plays to this very day and everything and everybody have to dance to his tune.

EIGHT

The Land of Youth

THERE ONCE LIVED a mighty King who in his younger days had led his army to many great victories over his enemies. The passing years had made him both older and wiser, and he now realized the folly of war. All he desired was a life of peace and contentment, for he was happy in the thought that his three sons would rule after him. In spite of his great age he remained unusually active until one day, suddenly, he was struck down by a mortal illness. For the first time in his life he became aware of death and a strange fear seized him. He summoned his wise men to the palace and told them he would sacrifice all he had if they would tell him how to prevent death; but they shook their heads sadly and went away.

As time went by the old King grew weaker, but his spirits rose when a fortune-teller, who had won fame in many lands, arrived in the capital. He immediately sent for her and said, 'Now I have been bedridden for many weeks and not even my wise men can help me. You are my only hope. Can you, old woman, tell me how I can defeat my last enemy which men call death?'

The old woman smiled and, laying a hand on his brow, said, 'Yes, I will tell you the secret of health and youth. Far, far away, many hundreds of miles from Denmark, there is a beautiful country. It is called the

Laying a hand on his brow she said 'Yes, I will tell you the secret of health and youth.'

Land of Youth. Here there flows a spring which never runs dry and near the spring grows an apple-tree; and nowhere else in the whole wide world can such beautiful apples be found. If you drink of the water from the spring and eat an apple from the tree, you will regain both your health and your youth. There are very few indeed who have tasted the water and the apples, however, for the way is long and fraught with danger.' This news cheered the King and the fortune-teller was well rewarded. Then, having wished him good-bye and good luck, she left the palace.

Soon afterwards the King called his eldest son to his bedroom and told him the fortune-teller's message. 'Go and find this wonderful land and bring me back water from the spring and apples from the tree,' he commanded the prince, giving him a large bag of money. The following day the prince set out on his journey, eager not only to save his father but for adventure in this strange new land. He had travelled for many days when he came to a busy city. Feeling hungry and weary, he went into the first inn he could see; but inside there were many temptations which he could not resist. He soon forgot his dying father and his errand, and from then on led a wild and reckless life.

The days turned into weeks and the weeks into months, and the old King grew impatient. Finally he could wait no longer and ordered his second son to go in search of the Land of Youth. With a bag of gold, the prince set out and after a few days he came to the same city as his brother. Like his brother, he stayed at the inn and he, too, fell to the temptations inside; and in his riotous living he forgot the water of life and the apples of youth.

A long time passed and the old King's servant kept watch at his bedroom window, hoping to catch sight of the prince; but as his son never came the King gave up hope and resigned himself to the end. The whole kingdom awaited with sorrow the news of his death.

The youngest prince was by now so tired of waiting for his brothers to return that one day he went to his father's bedside and begged to be allowed to go in search of the Land of Youth. He asked for money and, above all, for the King's blessing. His father was deeply moved and, smiling through his tears, said, 'I cannot let you go, my son, for now your two brothers are lost there would be no one to rule the country after me.' The young prince was so determined, however, that at last the King consented.

The prince took the same road as his brothers and eventually came to the inn. As he passed the windows his brothers beckoned him inside. They shouted and waved at him, but he pretended not to notice and continued on his journey.

Some days later the young prince was travelling through a great forest when darkness overtook him and he lost his way. He wandered around aimlessly and at last saw a light gleaming through the trees. He immediately walked towards it and soon came to a small hut where an old woman opened the door to him. She asked where he came from and what was his errand. He told her of his dying father and of his search for the Land of Youth where water from the spring restored health and apples from the tree gave eternal youth. The woman looked puzzled and said, 'Well, I have lived for three hundred years and no one has ever told me of this wonderful country; but I rule over all the beasts of the forest and tomorrow I will summon them here and ask them about it.' The prince thanked her, and having eaten a meal he went off to sleep for the night.

Early the following morning the old woman went

outside and played on her flute, and at once from all corners of the forest animals came scampering towards her cottage. When they were all gathered together she asked if any of them knew the way to the Land of Youth; but no one had ever heard of it. 'I'm afraid I can't help you,' said the old woman, 'but my sister who rules over all the birds of the air may be able to find out something. Climb on to the back of this wolf here and he will take you to her. Give her my regards, and good luck to you on your journey.' Thus the prince said good-bye and, having thanked the old woman for her trouble, set off on his journey. The road was long and difficult; up high mountains and down steep valleys the swift-footed animal took him.

Darkness had already fallen when the prince noticed a light in the distance. 'We shall soon be there,' said the wolf; and shortly afterwards they were inside the cottage of an old woman who was busily eating her supper. The prince told the old woman that her sister had sent him to inquire about the wonderful Land of Youth. She was astonished. 'I've never heard of that place!' she exclaimed, 'but perhaps my birds can help you.' Next morning she went outside and played her flute, and immediately all the birds of the air came winging their way towards her cottage. She asked them if they knew of the Land of Youth, but none of them could help. 'I am afraid I can't help you, then,' she said, 'but my sister who rules over the fishes and is three hundred years older than I, may have heard of it. My eagle will take you to her. Give her my regards and tell her I sent you.' Having thanked her, the prince climbed on to the eagle's back and waved good-bye.

The speed of the eagle as it flew over mountains and cities left the prince breathless. Afraid that the great height would make him faint and fall thousands of feet to the ground, he shut his eyes and held on for dear life. It was late in the evening that the eagle said, 'She lives just below us'; and at last the prince opened his eyes and saw through the blackness below him the twinkle of a tiny light. He was certainly relieved when, after a terrifying swoop, the eagle landed him just outside the cottage.

The prince told what his errand was and asked for shelter for the night. News of her two sisters pleased the old woman and she made him very welcome. However, her brow furrowed when he asked about the Land of Youth and she shook her head emphatically. 'No, I have never heard of that place before and I'm nine hundred years old,' she declared, 'but my fish may be able to help you. I will call them together tomorrow morning and we shall see.'

Early the next morning the old woman went down to the beach and played her flute, and immediately all the fish swam towards her. When they were all still she asked if any of them had heard of the Land of Youth. The fishes looked first at her and then at each other. No, they had never heard of that country. Suddenly the old woman cried out, 'What has happened to the old whale? He is nearly always first here. Can anybody see him?' The fishes all turned round, but not a sign could they see of him. They were just going to shake their heads when a mighty wave rolled towards them. The whale had come at last, two fountains of water spurting from his nostrils and his tail lashing the sea. The old woman was very angry with him. 'Why have you kept us waiting so long?' she demanded. The whale was sorry, he said, but when he heard the flute he had been far out at sea, in fact much farther than ever before. 'And where might that be?' the old woman inquired. 'I have been to a beautiful country called the

Land of Youth,' answered the whale; and all the fishes bobbed up and took notice.

The old woman, although secretly pleased, spoke severely to the whale. 'As punishment for being late, you shall take this prince straight back to this Land of Youth,' she commanded. The prince immediately clambered on to the back of the whale and they were off.

Not far from the beach is a wonderful palace . . .

The whale sped through the waves and did not stop until they reached the Land of Youth. Now it was dark, and before the prince waded ashore the whale said, 'If you want to return safely take good heed of my advice. Not far from the beach is a wonderful palace and in its garden you will find both the spring and the apples. All men and beasts are now asleep, but at midnight they will wake up again. Take an apple from the tree and fill your bottle with water and hurry back. Do not linger, for unless you are here before the clock strikes midnight, we shall both be killed.' The prince was grateful for this warning and promised not to loiter in the palace. As he walked towards the gates he saw lions, tigers, bears and dragons, all asleep. An eerie stillness had fallen over the palace and the prince hastened to complete his errand. Up the steps and through many fine rooms he ran. Never before, even in his own home, had he seen such beauty and such wealth. He paused for a few moments to admire the tapestries and paintings but, remembering the whale's warning, he hurried on. At last he came to the room which looked out upon the gardens, and soon he had reached the spring where the water sparkled crystal clear and the apples shone like gold. He listened to the strange music of the water as it splashed on the pebbles, and then bent to fill his bottle. He rose, caught hold of the overhanging branches of the tree and picked up as many apples as he could carry. Back he ran to the palace, intending to look again at the splendid halls. He went from room to room until he came to one more magnificent than all the others. He caught his breath, for there in the middle of the floor stood a bed, and in the bed lay a lovely woman, sound asleep. Never before had he seen such a beautiful maiden.

Heedless of the whale's advice, he could not resist lying by the side of the fair princess. He felt wonderfully happy and hoped the night would never end. At last the chimes of the palace clock told him that it was half past eleven. He must not delay. Immediately he kissed the maiden farewell and jumped up; but before leaving, he scratched his name on the wall above the princess's bed to remind her of his visit. Then he dashed off. He was only just in time. No sooner had he reached the sea-shore than a frightful noise caused him to shudder. The animals had woken up with savage roars and the armour of the knights clattered as they walked the palace grounds again. He was on the whale's back in a flash and away they went.

The whale at once dived under the water, and when he came to the surface again the prince, spluttering and trembling all over, asked him what he thought he was doing. 'You are not the only one to be frightened,' replied the whale. 'I felt just the same when you stayed to pick all those apples.' Some time later he dived again, deeper than before. When eventually they came to the surface the prince was so frightened that he could hardly keep a limb still. 'I was just as frightened myself when you rested on the princess's bed,' remarked the whale. They had not travelled much farther when the whale suddenly plunged below the waves for the third time. Down and down he dived and the prince's lungs reached bursting-point. He was terrified and thought his end had come. It seemed ages before they came to the surface again and he could breathe once more. 'You are a wicked whale to frighten me like that,' he gasped. 'I only wanted to teach you a lesson and make you realize how frightened I felt when you stayed to write your name on the wall in the princess's bedroom,' answered the whale.

After many hours the whale reached his home waters once more. The prince, eager to tell the Queen of the Fishes of his good fortune, bade the whale farewell and waded ashore. The nine-hundred-year-old woman was overjoyed to see him again and to hear his news. Then, to repay her for all she had done for him, the prince gave her an apple from the tree of youth and a sip of water from the spring of health. A wonderful change immediately came over her, and there before him stood a beautiful maiden. She hurried to her looking-glass, and when she saw that all her wrinkles had gone and that she now looked young and lovely, she thanked the prince over and over again. 'As a reward you may have this wonderful spur,' she said. 'When it is shaken it turns into a horse which will go wherever you wish and as fast as the wind.'

The prince thanked her and said good-bye. He went outside and shook his spur; and at once a magnificent horse stood before him. He sprang on to its back and raced off to the home of the Queen of the Birds. The six-hundred-year-old woman greeted him warmly and listened closely to all he told her. Grateful for the help she had given him, the prince gave her an apple and a sip of water; and there before him stood a lovely woman. The ruler of the birds looked into her mirror, and the expression on her face changed from amazement to joy. She went straight to her cupboard, took out a cloth and said, 'As a reward you may have this magic cloth. When you spread it out there will appear before you the finest foods and the choicest wines.'

The prince thanked her, and having said good-bye rode on to the home of the Queen of the Animals. The three-hundred-year-old woman was delighted to see him again and to learn that his errand had been successful. For her help he gave her an apple and a sip of water; and at once her wrinkles vanished, her back straightened and she stood there, radiantly beautiful as in the flower of her youth. This made her so happy that she gave the prince a jewelled sword with a golden hilt. 'Everyone and everything will fall back before you when you draw this sword,' she declared, 'whether it be the fiercest knight or the most savage beast.' The prince thanked her for this wonderful weapon and said good-bye. Fortune had indeed smiled on him and he hurried home to his father's palace.

He came at last to the city where his brothers were

leading their wild and reckless life. From the windows of the inn they saw him and called him inside to hear his story. They listened to all he had to say and praised him for his courage; but in their wicked hearts they were bitter and envious. Thus, when he had gone to bed and was sound asleep, they crept up to his room and stole the apples of youth and the water of health; and in their place they put apples from the tree at the back of the inn and water from the well in the yard outside.

The following morning the prince bade his brothers farewell, jumped on his horse and sped off towards his home. All the time he wondered whether he would be in time to save his dying father, and his heart beat anxiously. Finally he reached the palace where the old King rejoiced to see him again; and the prince thanked God for sparing his father until his return. He told the King of his wonderful adventure in the Land of Youth, and when he had finished he took out the apples and the water and bade his father taste them and become well again. With a trembling hand the old man drank from the bottle and ate the apples while the prince confidently awaited the outcome. But no change took place, and the old King lay as still and breathed as heavily as before. The prince looked puzzled and sad. Then he realized he had been tricked. But the old King, thinking his son had made a fool of him, grew so angry that he almost choked with rage.

The two elder brothers returned to the palace soon afterwards, shouting and laughing. They made their way to their father's bedside and boasted about their journey to the Land of Youth and the dangers they had braved. They gave the old King an apple from the tree of youth and water from the spring of health, and immediately a wonderful change occurred. His wrinkles disappeared, his grey hair turned golden and his blue

G

eyes sparkled. His strength returned and he jumped to his feet, young and handsome once more. He praised his two eldest sons for their courage and devotion, but his youngest son he despised; and so great was the wrath of the people against him that the King's Council sentenced him to be cast into the den of lions, and not even his father could save him.

The King's courtiers dragged him to the lions' den, threw him deep down into the pit and left him to his fate; but when the hungry animals rushed towards him the prince drew his sword and they backed away in fear; and with his magic cloth to help him he never went short of the finest food. Thus he passed seven long years and everyone thought him dead.

Meanwhile in the Land of Youth, the same year as the prince had visited the palace, there was born to the princess a beautiful baby son. He was perfect in every way except for a mysterious growth in the shape of an apple in the middle of his left hand. Doctors hurried to the palace but none of them dared cut it away. Finally, the worried princess summoned all the wise women in the land to tell her how this unsightly growth could be removed; and they agreed without exception that the child could only be cured when his rightful father had been found.

The years went by and the princess's little son grew up into a bright and lively youngster. On the day after his seventh birthday had been celebrated, the princess announced her intention to go in search of his father. Thus, every ship in her fleet was fitted with the strongest armour and the most skilful crews were chosen. She herself, accompanied by her little son, led the vessels out into the open sea in her own boat of solid gold. They sailed together far across the ocean to the kingdom of the prince who had written his name upon her bedroom wall. Many weeks later they reached their destination, and when the people in the capital saw the armada heading towards their own shore, there was great confusion and they all wondered who this strange enemy could be. The princess's ship sailed into the harbour and she immediately sent a message to the King, demanding to see his son who had been to the Land of Youth. The King replied that his eldest son would go down to meet her on the following day.

They sailed together far across the ocean . . .

The next morning the princess ordered a beautiful carpet, embroidered in gold, to be laid on the bridge of her ship; and there on her throne with her little son beside her, she awaited the arrival of the prince. It was noon when the prince rode down to visit her. He saw the fine carpet and rode on the right-hand side of it towards the princess; but he had gone no more than a few yards when the little boy cried out, 'That isn't my father!' And the apple-shaped growth on his hand remained as large as ever. So the prince returned to the palace, rejected and dishonoured.

The princess, thinking the King had deceived her, was so angry that she threatened to bombard the capital with red-hot cannon balls if the King failed to send on the following day his son who had visited the Land of Youth.

Next morning the King's second son went down to the harbour, and when he saw the magnificent carpet he rode on the left-hand side of it towards the princess. He had only gone half-way when the little boy shouted, 'That isn't my father'; and the growth showed no signs of disappearing. The princess now became so furious that she sent a message to the King by the prince, telling him that if on the following day his son who had visited the Land of Youth did not come to her boat, she would destroy the town and him as well.

The prince reported to his father what the princess had told him and the King paced up and down his room, baffled and worried. In despair he sent his messenger to the lions' den in the forlorn hope that his youngest son was still alive; and he was certainly amazed to learn that the prince had been seen, alive and well, and playing with the fierce beasts. But his son had insisted that the King himself must come to the lions' den and fetch him if he wished to save his people from the great danger which threatened them.

On the third day, arrayed in his finest clothes with his sword at his side, the young prince shook his spur and immediately before him appeared a magnificent horse, as fast as the wind. He swung himself into the saddle and rode along the main street. Everyone looked in wonder and admiration at this handsome rider on his wonderful steed. Straight down to the harbour he went and on to the boat. He rode along the middle of the gold-embroidered carpet at the end of which the princess and her son awaited him. As soon as the little boy caught sight of him he cried out, 'This is my father'; and that very moment the growth disappeared from his hand. The beautiful princess was overjoyed to find her son's father and her rightful bridegroom; and at once she fell in love with him. The crowds who thronged the quayside had never seen such a perfect match as their own handsome prince and this radiant princess.

To the cheering of the people and the ringing of bells the bride and bridegroom rode up to the town and on to the palace. The King was both relieved and happy and the wedding was celebrated with pomp and splendour. As for the two eldest brothers, they were thrown into the lions' den for their treachery; and they have never been heard of since. The prince, his bride and their little son returned, after the wedding, to the Land of Youth, and there they still live to this very day.

NINE

The Boy and the Mountain-Man

AMONG THE HEATHER on the wild moors of Jutland there stood a little cottage. Here, many years ago, lived a widow and her son, a ten-year-old boy. It was a hard and lonely life they led. Often when all seemed against them the woman would sit down and weep, but always her little boy put his arm around her and comforted her. 'If you can only wait until I grow up, then you will have some money,' he promised. But full of despair, she shook her head sadly. 'Times are bad, and money is so hard to come by, my son. I fear, like me, you will be poor all your days.' 'Not if I can help it,' replied the boy.

Their most treasured possession was an old sheep which every springtime had two lambs. The boy and his mother reared the lambs carefully for they provided wool for their clothes. One spring the woman had woven a fine piece of woollen cloth which she made into a dress. But the dress was so white all over that she couldn't possibly wear it, and she was too poor to afford to have it dyed in town. 'If only it were purple like the heather on the moors,' she sighed, 'then it would look really beautiful.' As she spoke she looked out of the window at the hills covered in heather on which the bright sun shone. The little boy would do anything to please his mother, and early the next morning with a

big sack and a few sandwiches, he set out on to the
moors to cut some heather so that she could dye her
dress. He walked over to the hill and soon he was cutting
the heather and putting it in his sack. But the sun was
high in the sky and its rays beat down on him. Soon it
was too hot for him to work, so he sat down on the hill-
top and ate his sandwiches. When he had finished he
lay back, and not long afterwards he had fallen fast
asleep. How long he slept he didn't know, but when at
last he awoke he started rubbing his eyes and looked
around him. Try as he might, he couldn't fathom out
where he was. Now the birds weren't singing any more,
there was no sun and his mother's hut had disappeared.
Around and above him were grey stone walls. He became afraid. 'Where am I?' he cried, and was startled
to hear a harsh voice reply, 'You are in the mountain-
man's den.' He turned round, and there in the corner
stood the mountain-man. His mother had often told him
stories about the mountain-man and his fear gradually
changed into curiosity.

'Won't you let me go home?' asked the boy at last.
'No,' replied the mountain-man, walking up to him.
'My wife and I need some help down here. We were
very lucky you came when you did, and had a sleep in
our house. You seemed such a big, strong lad that I
brought you down here, and now you can work for your
keep.' The boy thought it best to obey the mountain-
man and said he was willing to help all he could, but
secretly he planned to escape.

Now that day the mountain-man's wife intended to
brew beer, and so she asked her husband and the boy to
fetch some water, pointing to a huge vessel in the corner.
The boy went over to it to pick it up, but he soon found
out that it was all he could do to lift it when it was
empty, let alone when it was full of water. Breathing

heavily, he lowered the vessel as carefully as he could and gasped, 'Listen, master, why can't we fetch the well inside. Then we won't have to keep going out for the water?' 'What are you saying?' said the mountain-man, and ran out to his wife. 'Listen, wife,' he cried, 'the boy wants us to carry the well in here.' 'Such nonsense!' she exclaimed. 'If we bring all the water in here we shall be flooded out and drown. The silly fool!' Back went the mountain-man to the boy to tell him what his wife had said. 'Well, you'll have to fetch it yourself,' decided the boy, 'for it isn't worth going for so little water.' The boy seemed very angry and this frightened the mountain-man so much that he went himself and carried all the water his wife needed.

Later in the day his wife needed some peat. As before, the boy insisted on carrying the whole pile or none at all. But she only wanted a little peat and so the mountain-man had to carry it in himself.

That evening when they had all gone to bed, the boy tiptoed into their room to hear what they were talking about. From what they said he gathered that they were frightened of him. However, they dared not let him escape; nor did they want to keep him with them. Finally they decided to kill him when he was fast asleep. 'I'll see they don't,' thought the boy to himself, and returned to his own room. Suddenly his eyes fell upon an earthen pot full of butter. He picked it up and put it on his pillow while he, himself, crept under the bed. He was just in time. Only a few seconds later the mountain-man came in with a big hammer in his hand. He tiptoed up to the bed, lifted the hammer and brought it down with a stunning blow on the pillow where he saw vaguely what he thought was the boy's head. Instead, however, he hit the jar which splintered into a thousand pieces and the butter splashed all over the walls and ceiling. 'Well, did you manage to kill him?' asked his wife when the mountain-man returned to their room. 'I hit him so hard that I'll warrant there's not a whole bone left in his head,' answered the mountain-man, 'and the blood spurted all over the place.'

The boy waited until he heard the mountain-man snoring heavily and then he crept back into bed again. He slept soundly until the next morning when, very early, he went into the other bedroom and bade good morning to the mountain-man and his wife. Both of them opened their eyes wide in astonishment, and were too terrified to answer. The boy chuckled to himself and then asked when they were going to have breakfast as he was famished. At once the mountain-man's wife jumped out of bed and hurried to prepare some beer broth. While they were sitting at the table eating their breakfast, they tried to find out whether the boy had slept well. 'Yes, quite soundly,' replied the boy, 'although soon after I had gone to bed something seemed to fall from the ceiling, but it was probably just a dream.'

That night he tiptoed into the other bedroom again and listened in case they were hatching another plot against him. Indeed they were, but this time they planned to make him eat himself to death. Next morning the boy went outside and started looking in the rubbish heap. He searched until he found the mountain-man's old boots which he cleaned and hid under his jacket. Soon afterwards, breakfast was ready and the mountain-man and his wife made the boy eat as much gruel as he possibly could. Time after time his bowl was filled, and still the old woman added more. But she didn't notice that instead of going into his mouth, most of the gruel went into the top of the boots tucked away under the boy's chin.

While he ate, first the mountain-man and then his wife persuaded him to have more. At long last when they were convinced that the boy would soon split at the seams, the mountain-man finally helped himself to the last spoonful. Then they sat waiting for him to die.

. . . convinced that the boy would soon split at the seams.

But not a sign of dying did the boy show; in fact, he looked as well as ever. 'It's exercise that will finish him off,' thought the mountain-man; 'when he exerts himself he will probably burst.' So he suggested that they both enjoy themselves leaping over the stream which cut through the hill. The boy was eager for some fun and willingly agreed. The two then went outside to play.

Seeing the stream, the boy took a good long run, but pulled up suddenly on the near bank, pretending that it was too wide for him. When the mountain-man's turn came he, too, didn't feel inclined to jump, for he had eaten much more than usual. 'Listen,' said the boy, 'lend me your knife so that I can make myself a bit lighter. Then I shall clear the stream easily.' The mountain-man gave him his knife and the boy made long cuts under his jacket. But it was only the boots he slit, and the broth came pouring out. Then he jumped the stream without any difficulty. 'Why don't you try to make yourself lighter, too?' the boy suggested to the mountain-man. 'Do you think it's safe?' asked the mountain-man. 'Of course,' replied the boy, 'you'll be all right.' Reassured, the mountain-man took the knife and began cutting himself, and it wasn't long before he had fallen to the ground, dead. Back to the mountain-man's wife ran the boy and told her how wicked she and her husband had been; not only had they taken him away from his poor mother but they had also tried to kill him. 'As a punishment for your wickedness,' went on the boy, 'I have killed your husband and he now lies on the bank of the stream. Unless you show me the way out of this hill and give me all your gold and silver, you will suffer the same fate. Do you understand?' So terrified was the old woman that she hurriedly fetched her sack of gold and silver, helped the boy to lift it on to his back, and led him along the winding pathway through the hillside out into the fresh air once more.

The bright sunshine caused the boy to shield his eyes for a few minutes, but soon he grew accustomed to the daylight again. He looked around, saw the animals grazing near his mother's farm, and listened to the twittering of the birds near by. It was wonderful to be back. With all his money he made his way through the heather to his home where his mother waited anxiously for him. And from that day onwards they wanted for nothing.

TEN

King Find's Daughter

ONCE UPON A time in England there was a King who had an only son. Now one day this prince happened to see a picture of a Danish princess, and from then on he had no peace. At last he went up to his father and told him that he loved the Danish princess so much that he wanted to marry her. The King was greatly pleased, for he knew that if Denmark and England were united, no power on earth could conquer them. He thus wrote to the Danish King and demanded the latter's daughter for his son. The Danish King answered that his daughter had not yet grown up and, moreover, he had forbidden her ever to become Queen of England. This reply made the English King very angry and at once he wrote back, threatening war between the two countries unless the Danish princess became his son's bride. 'My daughter will never marry an English prince as long as a single Danish soldier has a drop of blood in his body,' replied the King of Denmark.

War followed. With a large army the English prince sailed to Denmark and besieged the capital. Secretly the Danish King sent his daughter to a small island and hid her inside a hill with seven maids, a little dog, and food for seven years. After that he had the hill walled up so that no one could reach her.

At the end of seven years the English prince had

conquered the capital and King Find, the Danish King, had been killed. The prince immediately began a search of the castle, and at last he came to the princess's room. In there he saw a loom made of ivory. Birds, fishes and all kinds of animals had been woven on the material, but the cloth was still unfinished. A long time had now passed since the prince had first sought the Danish princess and so he made known his intention to marry whoever could complete the work on the loom; for, he thought, when she realized she had nothing to fear and could become his bride, the Danish princess would come out of hiding.

Now one of the Danish dukes happened to have a daughter who was not only a clever weaver but the very image of the princess. He at once sent her to the castle to try her fortune. But the loom proved too complicated for her and everything she tried to weave went wrong.

Meanwhile, in the hillside on the island, the princess and her seven maids had eaten their seven years' provisions and now faced starvation. They tried in vain to break through the thick stone wall, and as the days went by they were nearly dying with hunger. At last one of the maids decided that she didn't want to live any longer, and she asked the princess to kill her and use her flesh for food. The princess carried out the maid's wish and ate her little by little. Not long afterwards another maid felt the same way and the princess ate her, too. One by one, all the maids wanted to die, and in the end only the princess remained. Soon she became so hungry that she was forced to eat the dog; but this did not satisfy her for long. Then she thought of an idea. The hill was full of rats and mice and so she caught and skinned them, and their bodies served as food for several days. In the meantime she had managed to break through the wall, and far out at sea she spotted a ship.

She immediately waved a white sheet to attract its attention, and when the vessel headed towards the island she sighed with relief.

During the seven years she had been on the island her once splendid clothes had turned to rags. Nevertheless, she returned to her former home, the castle, walked into the kitchen and asked whether they needed a maid for washing up. As she was very pretty the duke's daughter decided to give her a trial and she at once set to work. When Sunday came, the duke's daughter wanted water to wash herself, and the new maid took it up to the room which she, herself, once occupied. She looked around her and saw the loom just as she had left it over seven years ago. Noticing her interest in the loom, the duke's daughter said, 'That is the most difficult loom I have ever used!' 'If you will allow me, I will finish the cloth for you,' replied the maid. 'If you can, I will give you one hundred rigsdaler (one hundred florins) and after that I will make you my chambermaid,' promised the duke's daughter. The maid sat down at the loom, undid what the duke's daughter had woven wrongly and carried on with the pattern she had left seven years before. It did not take her long to finish, and as soon as she was gone the duke's daughter sent a message to the English prince to tell him that the work on the loom had been completed. Up came the prince, and finding nothing wrong with the cloth he kept his word and made arrangements to marry the duke's daughter; but in his heart he doubted whether she was the rightful princess.

Now the real Danish princess used to own a horse called Blanke which, having had to fend for itself during the seven war years, became so wild that two men had to pull it to the water to drink. The wedding had been arranged for the next Sunday and the English

prince decided that his bride should ride to church on
Blanke. The duke's daughter was terrified. So she said to
her chambermaid, 'If you'll ride to church on Blanke
in my place I'll pay you one hundred rigsdaler. We
look so much alike that no one will notice the difference.' The chambermaid agreed, knowing that the
horse would obey her.

Sunday came. The chambermaid took off her ragged
clothes and arrayed herself in the fine bridal gown.
Soon the prince arrived and took the chambermaid by
the hand and led her out into the castle courtyard where
Blanke stamped and kicked and bit. Quite calmly the
princess went up to him and said:

> 'Blanke, Blanke, kneel for me;
> It was I who last rode thee.'

As soon as the horse heard the voice of the princess it
became as meek as a lamb. It knelt for her and she
climbed on to its back. 'What did you say, my dear?'
asked the English prince. 'Nothing, my lord,' answered
the princess. They went on their way, but inwardly the
prince was pleased for he knew that no one but the
Danish princess would be able to ride Blanke.

At the drawbridge the Danish King's dog was tied.
There, howling and barking, it strained at its leash. It
was so fierce that everyone backed away from it. But
the princess went up to the dog and said:

> 'Dear dog, dear dog, bark not at me!
> King Find, my father, hath reared thee.'

The dog immediately recognized her voice and calmed
down. Then he jumped up and licked her hand. 'What
did you say, my dear?' asked the bridegroom. 'Nothing,
my lord,' answered the princess.

Outside the castle they came to a bridge which creaked and squeaked so dreadfully that they feared it might break under their weight. The princess stopped and said:

> 'O wide, wide bridge, creak not 'neath me,
> King Find, my father, hath built thee.'

Then the bridge became firm and still. 'What did you say, my dear?' asked the bridegroom as they passed over it. 'Nothing, my lord,' answered the princess.

They rode on until they came on to the wold. There the princess said:

> 'Here beneath the greenest wold
> The fishes swim so free and bold;
> If they had been in my hillside bare,
> I'd not have eaten my maids so fair.'

'What did you say, my dear?' asked the bridegroom. 'Nothing, my lord,' answered the princess.

Soon they were riding along the sea-shore and in the distance the princess saw the island where she had hidden during the war. Then she said:

> 'Out there the mice they were my meat,
> For they were all I had to eat.'

'What did you say, my dear?' asked the bridegroom. 'Nothing, my lord,' replied the princess.

At last they reached the church. Here the English prince took off his golden gloves and gave them to the princess who had to swear on her life to return them to none other than himself when he demanded them. When they arrived back at the castle from church, the princess went into the weaving room to change. But it was the duke's daughter who stepped out in her place to

H

see the bridegroom. The wedding feast was being prepared, but the prince was in no mood for celebrations and asked his guests to come back tomorrow to toast his bride and himself. Disappointed, the visitors departed.

When evening fell, the prince and the duke's daughter went together to the bridal chamber. There the prince asked her to repeat the words she had said before mounting the horse. The duke's daughter appeared quite flustered and answered, 'Oh dear! I don't know what can be the matter with me today. I keep forgetting everything. But I have a chambermaid and to her I have entrusted everything I have said. She is sure to remember it.' She hastened to the princess and said, 'What was it you said before you mounted Blanke?' The princess repeated the words, whereupon the duke's daughter ran back to the prince and said, 'Now I know; these are the words:

> Blanke, Blanke, kneel for me;
> It was I who last rode thee.'

'Yes, that's quite right,' said the prince, and the duke's daughter was quite pleased with herself. But then the prince asked her to repeat the words she had said when she came to the dog by the castle gate. 'Ah! I am so carried away by my love for you that today I can't think clearly, but now I'll go along to my maid and find out,' she replied; and as quickly as she could she ran to the princess. 'All the talk you have been doing on the way to church is driving me mad,' she grumbled. 'Now what is it you said to the dog?' The princess told her and back she went to the prince and said, 'These are the words:

> Dear dog, dear dog, bark not at me;
> King Find, my father, hath reared thee.'

'Quite right!' exclaimed the bridegroom. 'Upon my word, that is a wonderful chambermaid you have.'

The duke's daughter now thought everything was well and she was just going to settle down when the prince asked her the words she had said when they came to the bridge; and again she had to go and ask the princess. Then she repeated the words to the prince:

> 'O wide, wide bridge creak not 'neath me,
>   King Find, my father, hath built thee.'

'What a good memory your chambermaid has!' cried the prince. 'No doubt she will remember what you said when we rode over the wold.' So, however annoyed she might be with all this running backwards and forwards, the duke's daughter had to go again to the weaving room. 'What is it you've been talking about now, you hussy, when you rode with my husband over the wold?' Although she was most upset at the way the duke's daughter spoke to her, the princess humoured her mistress and told her the words. Back in the prince's room the duke's daughter said, 'Yes, now I remember clearly what I said. These are the words:

> Here beneath the greenest wold
> The fishes swim so free and bold;
> If they had been in my hillside bare,
> I'd not have eaten my maids so fair.'

'That's right,' said the prince. 'There is only one more question I want to ask you. What did you say when you saw the island out in the sea?' 'Oh dear!' replied the duke's daughter. 'I am so full of love for you that I forget everything else. But I repeated the words to my chambermaid when we came home from church and she will certainly remember them.' She hurried to the princess, much angrier than before. 'I can't understand the meaning of all that talking you did on the road. I'm sick to death of running backwards and forwards so many times to ask you. Now what did you say when you caught sight of the island?' she demanded. Meekly, the princess told her. Knowing this was the last question, the duke's daughter returned to the bridegroom full of smiles and said, 'These are the words I spoke:

> Out there the mice they were my meat,
> For they were all I had to eat.'

'That maid has a memory for both of you!' declared the prince.

The duke's daughter now thought they could settle down for the night, but then the prince said, 'Now will you give me back those golden gloves I gave you.' 'I've hidden them in my chamber, but I will go and fetch them at once,' she answered. She went straight to the princess, and this time she asked for the prince's gloves most politely. She was certainly taken aback when the princess replied, 'No! I have sworn on my life that I, myself, and no other, will give him back the gloves.' The duke's daughter wrung her hands in desperation for she was baffled over what to do next. Suddenly the princess had an idea. 'We will go together to his chamber. I will put out the light and give the prince his gloves in the dark. Then I will hurry outside and you can stay with him,' she suggested. 'I am sure he won't know who has given him the gloves.'

Thus they went to the prince's room. As soon as they were inside, the princess put out the light, went up to the prince and handed the gloves to him. She was just going to rush out when the prince seized her arm and held her tight. 'You who have given me my gloves must stay with me,' he cried, 'and whoever else is in the room must go.'

Next morning the duke's daughter was sent back to her family, and, with great joy, guests from far and near toasted the English prince and his Danish bride.

ELEVEN

The Rich Per Muller

THERE WAS ONCE a rich Danish innkeeper by name of Per Muller. Judging by the number who sat every night on the wooden benches along the walls of his bar, his inn was very popular. Late one evening when the room was crowded, a strange old man entered and sat on the bench. He was followed shortly afterwards by a poor married couple who asked for shelter since the woman expected her baby at any moment. 'Sit down on this bench,' offered the rich Per Muller, 'this is all the room we have left.' But when she was to bear her child she couldn't sit on the bench any longer, so Per Muller said, 'We have no other place in the house except the big oven.' The wife was thus obliged to go into the oven where she gave birth to her son. Meanwhile in the bar all they could talk about was the poor woman in the oven. After listening to what the others had to say, the strange old man startled everyone by prophesying that, when he grew up, the little boy lying in the oven would marry the rich Per Muller's only daughter.

Now Per Muller, who was lying in bed, overheard what the strange man said and became very angry. 'That's a lie. I'll see to it he doesn't marry my daughter,' he thought to himself. A few days later the poor woman was ready to set off with her husband and child. They were about to leave when Per Muller confronted them saying, 'You are so poor, it must be all you can manage to look after yourselves; now you have a child, life will be much harder. I've been thinking things over and, if it will help you, I will look after your son for you. You may be quite sure he will be well provided for and I shall love him as if he were my very own.' Thinking their little boy would grow up to enjoy wealth and opportunities which

. . . there came through the wood a rich man followed closely by
a poor man

otherwise would be denied him, the couple were happy to accept the offer and went off, leaving their little baby behind. No sooner had they disappeared, however, than the rich Per Muller poked out both the little boy's eyes and threw him into a thicket deep in the wood.

That same day at eventide there came through the wood a rich man followed closely by a poor man. Suddenly the latter shouted to the one in front, 'I wonder what that screaming is ahead of us.' 'It's probably a carcass that the ravens are pecking at,' replied the rich man, and on they went. The poor man, however, grew more and more puzzled and, tethering his horse to a tree, he ran deep into the forest to find out what was happening. It was there where the shrubs were thickest that he found the child. Hurriedly he picked it up, wrapped it in some old rags and rode home with it. His wife who had no children of her own was so happy to see the boy, but when she saw that his eyes had been poked out she became very sad. Feeling sorry for the little one, the man and the woman kept the boy and brought him up as if he were their own child.

One spring they happened to have good luck with their goslings, but the poor blind boy could not look after them as he trod on them and killed them. Thus, in order to tend to the birds they had to hire a peasant girl, and when she took the goslings into the fields the boy used to go with her. One day while they were out together the strange old man from Per Muller's bar came up to him, stroked his cheek and passed his hand over his eyes. 'Now I can see!' suddenly exclaimed the boy, who was so happy that he ran straight home to his foster-parents who were as delighted as he. Now the rich Per Muller had long since heard talk of the blind boy whom the poor people had found and it occurred to him that this was probably the boy he had tried to get rid of some years previously. One day he called at the poor people's cottage and said, 'I am on a long journey, but I have forgotten to tell my wife some business that must be attended to while I am away. Will your little boy take a letter to my wife?' 'Most certainly,' replied the man, 'but he probably won't know the way as it is only recently that he regained his sight. Still, he has a tongue in his head and can ask if he goes wrong.' The rich Per Muller quickly scribbled a note to his wife telling her to keep the boy until the oven was red hot, and then she was to throw him inside and burn him up. The boy set off with the letter, but on his way he met the strange old man who asked to read the message he was carrying. The boy showed him the note. Having read it, the strange man went over the handwriting with his finger and then directed him to the inn. Here Per Muller's wife opened the door to him and read the letter. She saw that her husband had asked her to receive the boy well and care for him as though he were her own son. She did as her husband commanded, bought the boy fine clothes and looked after him well. Some days later the rich Per Muller came home. The first thing he saw was the little boy looking so happy and well. 'Why haven't you done what I told you?' he stormed at his wife. 'I did exactly as you wrote,' she protested and showed him the letter; there, written in his own hand, he read that his wife was to receive the boy well and be kind to him. Rich Per Muller soon began to fathom out how he could get rid of the boy. 'Listen my boy,' he said at last, 'will you go on an errand for me?' 'Certainly,' replied the boy. 'I want you to go to Hell,' said Per Muller, 'and ask the Devil how long I still have to live.'

The boy immediately got ready to begin his journey. On the way he went through a country which had a severe drought. Here the King sent for him and asked, 'Will you take a message to Hell and find out from the Devil the meaning of this drought we're having, and how we set about getting water?' 'Certainly,' replied the boy, and on he walked. Later he came to another country where the King also sent for him and asked him to take a message to Hell. 'In the garden we have an apple-tree which used to bear gold and silver apples,' he said sadly, 'but now it is barren. Ask the Devil how this came about and how we can make the tree bear golden apples as before.' 'I will,' replied the boy, and continued on his way. Eventually he came to the third kingdom where there was great sorrow, for the King's daughter had become leprous when she went to make her communion for the first time. The King asked the boy to find out how this came about and how he could make his daughter well again. The boy said that he would do so and hurried off on the long walk to Hell.

But even the longest road comes to an end and at last the boy arrived at a great river where a ferryman rowed him across to Hell. Before the boy went inside Hell, however, the ferryman said, 'Tell the Devil I'm heartily sick of waiting by this river and ferrying people across. I've been doing this for three hundred years and I'd like to know how I can get away from here.' 'I'll see to that,' promised the boy and then entered the black gates of Hell. It was the Devil's great-grandmother who received him for the Devil was not at home. He told her everything that he was to ask the Devil, and after he had finished his story she said, 'I will do my best, but I am afraid an ill fate lies in store for you. When the Devil comes home you had better creep under the bed and keep quite still. Listen carefully to every word the Devil says in answer to my questions.' The boy was relieved now the Devil's great-grandmother intended to help him, so he crawled under the bed and lay as still as a mouse. Shortly afterwards the Devil came home. Snorting and groaning, he cried, 'I can smell Christian blood here, great-grandmother.' 'Don't worry about that,' she replied, 'that's only the raven who flew over our house with the bones of a Christian in his mouth. One of the bones dropped down the chimney and burnt. That's what you can smell.' This explanation appeared to satisfy the Devil who went to bed followed by his great-grandmother.

The Devil had not slept long before his great-grandmother shouted, 'Ah! I dreamt, I dreamt.' 'Well, what did you dream?' asked the Devil. 'I dreamt the rich Per Muller inquired how long he had still to live,' replied his great-grandmother. 'I could easily tell you that, but I can't see why that concerns you,' said the Devil. 'Oh, yes, it does,' went on his great-grandmother, 'I should just love to know.' 'Ah, well, I suppose I can tell you,' confided the Devil, adding, 'The rich Per Muller isn't going to die at all, but is going to live for ever after.' Then the Devil had peace of mind and fell asleep again. Not long afterwards, however, he was awakened by his great-grandmother shouting, 'Ah! I dreamt, I dreamt.' 'Well, what did you dream?' asked the Devil. 'I dreamt that the King in that country where they have a great drought asked how it came about and what he was to do to get water again.' 'I could easily tell you,' replied the Devil, 'but I can't see how it concerns you.' 'Oh, yes, it does,' said his great-grandmother, 'I should love to know.' 'All right, I suppose I'll tell you,' replied the Devil. 'Outside the town lies a huge stone. When it is lifted half-way up, water will come to all springs and wells, but if it is lifted all the way up, the whole country will be flooded.' The Devil then had peace of mind again, but it wasn't long before his great-grandmother cried, 'Ah! I dreamt, I dreamt.' 'What did the dream say?' inquired the Devil. 'I dreamt that the King with the golden apple-tree asked what he must do to make his tree bear gold and silver apples as before.' 'I could easily tell you, but I can't see what it matters to you,' replied the Devil. 'I don't suppose it does,' said his great-grandmother, 'but I should love to know.' 'All right, I suppose I'll tell you,' said the Devil. 'It's happening because a viper has wound itself round the root of the tree. If the King can get the viper off, it will bear gold and silver apples as before.' So saying, the Devil dropped off to sleep again only to be roused by his great-grandmother's voice. 'Ah! I dreamt, I dreamt,' she cried. 'What did you dream?' asked the Devil. 'I dreamt that the King of the country where the princess became leprous when she made her first communion asked me how it came about and what he was to do to make her well again.' 'I could easily tell you,' said the Devil, 'but I can't see that it matters to you.' 'I don't suppose it does,' replied his great-grandmother, 'but I should love to know.' 'All right, I may as well tell you,' said the Devil, 'it has happened because she dropped the wafer when she was making communion, and a big frog snatched it and crept under the altar; and there he still sits with the wafer in his mouth. When the King breaks up the altar, recovers the wafer and lets the princess eat it, she will get well again.' With this information the great-grandmother let the Devil go to sleep again, but not for long did she give him peace. 'Ah! I dreamt, I dreamt,' she shouted. 'Well, what did you dream about this time?' asked the Devil. 'I dreamt that the ferryman by the river told me that he was sick of rowing people across to Hell. He has done it now for three hundred years and he wanted to know how he could get away from there,' answered his great-grandmother. 'I could easily tell you that, but I don't see that it concerns you,' said the Devil. 'I don't suppose it does,' went on his great-grandmother, 'but I should just love to know.' 'All right,' said the Devil, 'I will tell you just this once, then you must leave me in peace. All he has to do to become free is to catch someone else and put him this side of the river and say, "Now you're the ferryman in place of me." Then he will be able to go wherever he wants.'

The boy now had all the information he needed and the Devil and his great-grandmother settled down to sleep in earnest. He got up early next morning and tip-toed outside. 'Hurry up!' whispered the Devil's great-grandmother, 'and remember all you have heard.' 'I certainly shall,' replied the boy gratefully. 'There is one more thing I must tell you,' added the Devil's great-grandmother, 'you must not tell the ferryman how to become free until you are on the other side of the river.' 'I certainly won't,' answered the boy, and set off on the long journey home. When he reached the river the ferryman said, 'Have you a message for me?' 'Yes, I have,' replied the boy, 'but I shan't tell you until you have ferried me across the water.' The ferryman rowed the boy over the river and when he was safe on the other bank the boy told him how he could become free. 'I wish that I'd known that before,' groaned the ferry-man, 'then you could have stayed here in my place.'

But the boy was happy to have escaped and hurried off. Soon he came to the kingdom where the princess was leprous. Up to the King he went and told him how to cure his daughter. The King, as you would expect, did not take long to break up the altar and, sure enough, there under it lay the frog with the wafer in its mouth. The princess ate the wafer and immediately became well and healthy again. There was no end to all the good things the King wanted to do for the boy who had brought him back this blissful message from the Devil. He lavished gold and many wonderful presents upon him, and the boy, no longer poor, travelled on happily. Next he arrived in the country where the apple-tree would not bear gold and silver fruit. Hearing what the boy said, the King at once ordered his gardener to dig under the tree, and the viper which had wound itself round the roots was killed; immediately the tree started to grow buds again. When the King saw buds all over his precious apple-tree, he was so pleased that he gave the boy a vast sum of money and made him a Duke. The boy was now so rich and important that he didn't walk any more but drove in splendour to the third kingdom. Here the King lifted the stone half-way and at once water came to all the springs and wells; and here the Duke received even more money than in the other two countries, for not only had he helped the King but the entire population as well, and all of them wanted to show their gratitude towards him.

The poor blind boy had now become rich and influential, and went everywhere with pomp and ceremony. One day he halted his golden coach in front of rich Per Muller's inn and bade his servants run in and inquire whether the innkeeper would receive him. Rich Per Muller, hat in hand, came to the door himself, apologizing profusely because his house was not fine enough to receive such an important visitor; but the Duke brushed aside his excuses, saying, 'Nevertheless, I'll still come in and you can serve me the best you have.' Beer and the finest food that could be provided were served on the table, and the rich Per Muller's own daughter waited on them. When they had finished their meal, the Duke said to Per Muller's daughter, 'Now what can I give you for all your trouble? I know of nothing better to offer you than myself.' Per Muller opened his eyes wide when he heard that the rich and influential Duke wanted to have his daughter, and soon everything was settled between them. Then they started sending out invitations to the wedding. When all the wealthiest and most important people were invited, the Duke said, 'Now you must also invite the poor people who were foster-parents to the boy who couldn't see'; and it was no use the rich Per Muller cringing and refusing to have such poor people! The Duke insisted, and they came to the wedding with all the greatest and richest in the kingdom. When they were going into the wedding feast, the bridegroom asked them to sit next to him at the top end of the table, and, although he certainly didn't like it, Per Muller had to give way to his influential son-in-law.

While the dinner was in progress, rich Per Muller looked around him and said scornfully, 'Here you can see what use prophecies are. Many years ago a strange man prophesied that my daughter would marry a poor boy born out there in my oven.' Hearing this, the bridegroom immediately stood up and answered, 'Here you can see what use prophecies are, for I am the poor boy born in the oven, and I am the boy you sent to Hell to ask how long you still had to live. The Devil told me that you would never die but live for ever.' The rich Per Muller jumped for joy when he heard this and cried, 'If you can make such a lot of money going to Hell, I will go on my way at once.' 'By all means,' said the bridegroom, 'off you go!' Per Muller immediately set

off for Hell. Through the three kingdoms he travelled, but nobody asked him to take a message to the Devil. At last he arrived at the river before Hell. Without a moment's hesitation the ferryman grabbed the rich Per Muller and put him to the oars, at the same time jumping ashore himself. There the rich Per Muller had to remain, and he is probably there to this very day.

TWELVE

The Three Princesses

IT WAS WINTER long ago. The King and Queen were out riding in their sleigh when suddenly the Queen's nose started to bleed and the blood dripped red on the newly-fallen snow. Then she wished that she might have a daughter as beautiful as the snow and the blood. At the same moment an old woman appeared beside her and said, 'Your wish shall be fulfilled. A daughter as beautiful as snow and blood will be born to you, but you must guard her well. Never allow her outside the palace for a single second until her seventh birthday or a terrible misfortune will befall you.'

Exactly a year later the King and Queen were out riding in their sleigh in the open countryside. Again the Queen's nose bled and she made the same wish as before. Immediately the old woman stood at her side again and told her the wish would be fulfilled.

The following winter the same incident happened for the third time, and each year the Queen gave birth to a beautiful baby daughter.

The three princesses were their mother's pride and joy. She watched over them day and night with all her care and love and would never leave them. Finally, feeling that life was too hard for her, the King tried to persuade her to go out and enjoy herself occasionally, for his faithful servants would guard the children with their lives. But the Queen would not be tempted; her greatest pleasure and happiness came from looking after her three daughters, and not until they reached the age of seven would she leave them. No trouble was spared to enable the three princesses to enjoy themselves within the palace, but never were they allowed to set so much as a foot outside. With longing and sadness in their eyes they often looked out into the garden and asked, 'Mother, shall we never be able to go out there?' 'Yes,' replied the Queen, 'as soon as you are seven years old, you may play outside as long as you wish.'

Now the youngest of the three sisters was the loveliest, and she it was who longed most to go outside. She wanted so much to play with the little boy who walked about in the garden and did the odd jobs. He was a poor and lonely lad whom the King had found on his travels; but he was so handsome that he could easily be mistaken for a prince. On Sundays, dressed in his best clothes, the little boy came and played with the youngest princess: and their favourite game was called 'Rolling Golden Apples'. They were so happy playing together, for whatever pleased the princess also pleased the little boy. When one Sunday had gone, they looked forward eagerly to the next. In this way time slipped by until the eldest daughter was nearly seven, and the youngest nearly five.

Now at this time in one of the great cities of the kingdom there happened to be an important celebration to which the King and Queen were invited. Knowing his wife's thoughts and feelings, the King tried hard to persuade her to attend, for, he said, his people would be deeply disappointed if she stayed at home and, after all, the happiness of their subjects should be their first concern. Finally, but reluctantly, the Queen agreed.

To calm the Queen, the King went to great trouble

to ensure that their children should come to no harm while they were away from the palace. Their oldest and most faithful servant was to care for them and he swore that he would take his own life if anything happened to the princesses. At last the great day came and the King and Queen drove off in splendour to the distant city.

When her parents had gone, the youngest princess sat on a velvet cushion by the open window from where she could look out on the palace garden. Of course, all she could think about was the little boy, and when she caught sight of him she beckoned him to come and play with her; and a lovely time they had, throwing apples in and out of the window. Eventually, the youngest princess asked the servant if she might go out into the garden to play with the kind little boy just for a few minutes. At first the old man shook his head, but when the two elder princesses begged to go outside as well and when the nursemaid said she could see no harm in it, he gave them permission. The little girls jumped for joy. All they wanted to do, they said, was to play rolling the golden apples for a little while, and then they would come indoors.

So, with the old servant in front and the nursemaid behind, the little princesses went out into the garden for the first time in their lives. The sun was shining and the birds were singing; everything was so peaceful that nothing could possibly happen to the children. They ran straight to the lawn, chatting excitedly. Just as they reached where they intended to play, however, there came a terrible storm followed by a whirlwind. The old servant and the nursemaid shielded their eyes from the force of the gale, but when after a few moments it had passed and they looked around them, the three little princesses had gone. Through the palace grounds they looked, in every bush and tree, but all in vain. Then came the sentries and the other servants to help them, and no one searched more eagerly than the little boy. Finally they gave up, and the old servant, fearing the wrath of his master, fled the country.

Everybody mourned the loss of the sweet little princesses, but most grief-stricken of all was the Queen. It was her fault, she insisted, for this would not have happened if she had stayed at home to guard the children until they were seven years old. With all her heart she wished that she could die. She immediately had a black dress made of the thickest silk and said that she would not take it off as long as it held together; but if her daughters did not return before it was worn out, grief would bring her to her grave. Although the King, too, had a heavy heart, he carried on with his daily work as bravely as he could. Everything possible was done to cheer up the Queen and to make her forget the princesses, but it was of no avail. Finally, to console themselves, she and the King decided to adopt the foundling with whom the little princess used to play.

Some years later the soldiers of their enemies poured over their frontiers. At once the King marched off at the head of his army and won a great victory; and none fought more valiantly than the boy who was now looked upon as the King's son.

When the triumphant warriors returned home the boy asked the King if they could mark their victory by a great celebration; but the King refused. 'Not until the princesses return shall there be any feasting and rejoicing,' he vowed, and promised that if the boy found and saved his three daughters he could take the little Lise, with whom he once played, as his bride.

'I shall try when I am a little older,' answered the King's son. 'Very well,' said the King, 'but I beg of you not to delay too long for the Queen's dress will not last much longer, and when it is worn out, her death will follow.'

What the King had said weighed heavily on the boy, and from then on he thought only of the princesses and of how to save them. One night he dreamt that the King had given him a suit of armour and a horse; he rode with two other men until he reached a vast forest in a foreign country where he found and saved the princesses who were imprisoned in a bewitched palace. What happened afterwards, however, faded with his dream.

The following morning he told the King of his dream and said that he intended to ride until he found both the forest and the palace. This pleased the King and at once he told the Queen, but, to his great disappointment, she was opposed to the idea, saying that their son would probably never return, and that would only add to their sorrow. 'As a matter of fact,' she went on, 'I don't want my daughters back any more, for my dress has nearly worn out and soon I shall be going to join them.' She was silent for a moment and then added, 'Our son won't find them for they are dead and gone. I beg of you not to let him go.' Time and time again the King tried to persuade the Queen to change her mind, but in vain. Then he had an idea. He went to her one morning and said that he had to send an urgent message to the King of a neighbouring country, and none less than their own son could deliver it with two noblemen as his companions.

To this the Queen consented and the King's son was equipped with horse and armour exactly as he had seen them in his dream. Two of the King's faithful courtiers volunteered to go on the journey, but really they were envious of the poor boy who had become a prince and hoped to get rid of him, feathering their own nest at the same time. In order to help them on their way the King gave them four purses of gold, two for his son and one for each of his companions.

The three rode for many months until at last their food was gone and their purses empty. The two courtiers were now so discouraged that they wanted to return home, but the King's son insisted on carrying on until they reached their goal. Finally, far away, the prince caught sight of the forest he had seen in his dream and they rode swiftly towards it. Once inside the forest, they each decided to take a different path, and if one of them needed help he was to blow his hunting horn.

Not long afterwards the King's son came across a palace, almost in ruins. He rode round to the back of the building, tied his horse to a tree and went inside. The first room he entered was evidently the kitchen as a large pot of soup was boiling away on the fire. Convinced that the princesses were hidden here, he ran outside and sounded his horn. His companions soon arrived and he asked them to help him search the old palace. They were desperately hungry, however, and when they saw the soup bubbling they couldn't resist pouring some out into their bowls. Then, just as they were going to eat, they saw a human hand floating in the pot, and at once they dropped their spoons in horror. Their hunger was now so intense that they decided to go at once into the forest to hunt deer; and the King's son was left to search for the princesses alone.

The two courtiers had only been gone a few seconds when into the kitchen stepped a big troll. With an ugly grin he licked his lips and exclaimed, 'You'll make some lovely soup for me!' 'Don't be greedy! Eat what you have in the pot first!' the King's son answered. 'No, I want to make sure of you,' said the troll. 'You won't find me as easy to have as all that,' the King's son challenged, drawing his sabre. The troll at once brushed the weapon aside, crying, 'That won't hurt me!' Then, seizing the King's son, the troll dragged him to the chopping block and ordered him to lay his head on the block. The King's son remained very calm meanwhile and said, 'I would help you if only I knew what to do. Just show me where to put my head and then I'll do as you say.' 'All

. . . the troll dragged him to the chopping block.

right, then,' the troll agreed; 'as it's your last wish I'll do as you ask.' Then the troll knelt on the floor and leaned over the block. 'This is all you have to do!' he explained. 'I'm afraid I still don't understand,' replied the King's son. 'Lie down properly!' Irritated by the other's stupidity, the troll stretched himself out full length with his head on the block, and like lightning the King's son grabbed the axe and struck with all his might; and the troll's head rolled across the kitchen floor.

That very moment there was an ear-rending crash and the bewitched palace had gone. The King's son found himself standing on a steep hill. Near by was an entrance and when he peered inside, it was as though he were looking down into a chimney, only infinitely longer and as black as pitch. At once he blew his horn and the other two came galloping back with a hare they had shot. Soon the animal had been roasted and they were enjoying a tasty meal. After they had eaten, the King's son asked his companions if they would climb down the pit to search for the princesses, but they couldn't be persuaded or even bribed, and in the end he had to go himself. Having tied ropes securely around his waist, the two companions edged him over the entrance inch by inch into the depths below.

At last he reached the bottom and inky blackness. High above him he could dimly discern the tiny stars. He groped his way along a passage until he came to a door. He knocked, and when it opened there stood before him three girls, all fully grown and beautiful. 'These are undoubtedly the missing princesses,' he thought. After he had greeted them he asked if they could remember the little boy who did the odd jobs in the palace garden and who played 'Rolling Golden Apples'. At once they recognized him, and when they learnt that he had come to rescue them they were overjoyed; and the youngest of the princesses was so happy that she flung her arms around his neck and kissed him. Suddenly they remembered the troll and their joy turned again to sadness. He was so strong, they said, that no one could possibly kill him. 'You need never fear him again for he has been killed,' the King's son replied. 'Now we must hurry and get away from here as soon as we can.' When they had collected their few belongings, the King's son signalled to his companions who pulled up the three princesses, one by one, to safety. Before his own turn came, however, he tied the rope round a large stone, as he suspected that the courtiers wanted to get rid of him. It was exactly as he had thought. The stone was only half-way up the pit when it came hurtling down again, clattering on the hard floor. Had the King's son been at the end of the rope, his death would have been certain. He sighed with relief.

At the top of the pit the two scoundrels pretended that it had all been an accident and professed their innocence while the princesses wept bitterly, refusing to leave until the King's son had been rescued. The two companions insisted that it was impossible to save him and finally the princesses had to agree to return home. Moreover, the sisters were forced to promise that they would tell their parents that it was the courtiers who had saved them from the troll, and that they had never even set eyes on the King's son.

While the wicked courtiers and the three princesses travelled home together, the King's son paced up and down, hopelessly beaten. Soon he felt hungry, and when he searched around him he found only enough food for three days. He ate his fill and his courage returned. On he went, farther into the hill until he reached the troll's den. Here he noticed a bottle marked 'Troll's strength'. He looked at it, deep in thought. If he took a sip he would probably become strong enough to climb out of the hill. 'No,' he decided at last, 'I should be like a troll all my life if I drank that.' Suddenly an idea occurred to him: why couldn't he climb out of the hole in the same way as a sweep gets up a chimney? He must hurry if he was to catch up with the princesses before they

reached the palace, for no doubt the two courtiers would
force them to lie to the King and Queen.

He tied his sword at his hip, commended himself to
God's safe keeping and started his long climb. This was
undoubtedly the hardest task he had ever faced. For two
whole days and a night he crawled upwards, but the end
was still far off. The thought of the youngest princess
spurred him on to greater efforts, but at last his courage
and his strength began to fail. The realization that he
was slipping back and losing as much ground as he had
gained made his heart sink. In despair he prayed that
the God who had given him life and favoured him with
fortune, who had guided and guarded him until that
very day, might now help him in his peril and, miracu-
lously, with a mighty heave he found himself on the top
of the hill. He was soon riding homewards, happy and
carefree again.

When after several days he reached the capital, he
saw that every house was decorated with flowers and
flags, and that everyone was gay and excited. He soon
discovered the reason. That same day his two companions on the journey were to marry the two youngest
princesses. At once he took off his suit of armour and
put on a completely new attire so that no one would
recognize him. Boldly he walked into the palace, intro-
ducing himself as a prince from a foreign country. 'We
are indeed fortunate to have you call upon us!' exclaimed the old King. 'We need just one more bridegroom for my eldest daughter.' Then the two went together to the banqueting hall where the Queen, robed in
red and white and happy once more, offered the strange
prince her hand. 'Although our happiness is not complete, we must be thankful that our real children have
returned,' she said, and sighed sorrowfully for their lost
son. As the Queen was speaking the two bridegrooms

eyed the stranger suspiciously while the youngest princess, a bridal wreath around her neck, blushed all over. At the same time the two eldest princesses nodded to her, and the Queen, noticing their strange behaviour, looked puzzled and annoyed. As a matter of fact she had very mixed feelings over the wedding for, since it had been arranged, her daughters – and especially the youngest – had been miserable and sullen. Now the princesses were staring at the stranger, their faces flushed with excitement. Since the strange prince had entered the hall everyone had been quiet. He had spoken of the great happiness which the return of the princesses must have brought to the King and Queen; but when he stopped talking everyone else was silent too. Feeling embarrassed, he suggested that everybody should tell a fairy tale. The idea was welcomed and everyone looked to the old King to begin; but when the King insisted that he never had been any good at telling stories, all eyes turned on the foreign prince.

The stranger told his own fairy tale, of how with two courtiers he had gone in search of three princesses who had been taken to a castle in a dense forest; of how he had chopped off the troll's head and of how, just as he had rescued the princesses, his companions had betrayed him. When he came to the very place in the story that we ourselves have reached, he startled everyone by showing some of the things he had brought from the troll's den.

The youngest princess could contain herself no longer. She jumped to her feet, flung her arms around the stranger's neck and kissed him. 'This is the one who killed the troll and saved us while these men here left him in the pit to die and made us lie to our parents,' she cried, pointing her finger at the two bridegrooms.

'Yes, every word our sister has said is true,' said the other two princesses together.

The King now turned his wrath upon the two courtiers and asked if they had anything to say, but their only response was to droop their heads and beg forgiveness. 'It is for my daughters and my adopted son to decide what shall be your fate,' declared the King. The King's son suggested that they should be banished from the country for ever, but the princesses insisted that they should be hanged as they had really been guilty of betraying the trust of the King himself; and this sentence was carried out immediately. The old-saying that 'whoever is unfaithful to the King must marry the gallows', was thus observed.

The wedding between the youngest princess, Lise, and the King's son, who once did odd jobs at the palace, took place the same day, and they now play 'Rolling Golden Apples' in the garden to their hearts' content.

THIRTEEN

Lazy Hans

THERE WAS ONCE a woman who had a lazy son. His name was Hans, and although fourteen years old and a big hefty lad, he couldn't be bothered to do anything – no, not a thing would he do. One day his mother said to him, 'Hans, will you go down to the sea-shore to fetch a bucket of water for me?' 'I'm too tired,' yawned Hans. But that day his mother was in no mood to put up with her son's idleness. She picked up the poker and, waving it in the air, shouted, 'If you won't go this very minute I'll teach you a lesson you won't forget, my lad.' Hans saw that his mother meant business and immediately took the bucket and went off. Not being used to work, however, he soon began to feel tired, and turning his bucket upside down he sat on it to rest. After a few minutes he went on, but only ten steps later he felt tired again and had to rest. In this way, stopping every few steps, he eventually reached the sea-shore. Here he dropped the bucket into the water, waited a few minutes and then pulled it out. What a pleasant surprise he had, for inside the bucket was a lovely little goldfish! 'Mother will be pleased when she knows I've caught a fish for her,' thought Hans. He was just about to return home when the goldfish suddenly started to talk, and begged the boy to put it back into the sea again. 'Oh, no, I

won't!' replied Hans, 'you got into the bucket without
my help and there you'll stay. I can't be bothered to
throw you back.' 'Please let me go,' pleaded the goldfish. 'Then you may have three wishes fulfilled.' Hans
brightened up at this and said, 'All right, but you'll have
to jump out of the bucket into the water yourself for I
am too tired to lift you.' With a jump the fish was out
of the bucket and into the sea, and was soon swimming
about happily again. Having watched it swim off, Hans
decided to have one of his three wishes. First he wished
he had a lovely sleigh without horses to drive him home
with his bucket of water. No sooner had he spoken than
there appeared before him a sleigh, all spick and span
and ready to drive off. As soon as he was sitting
inside with his bucket beside him, the sleigh moved
off like lightning, and Hans was so thrilled that he
forgot all about the other two wishes which were due
to him.

On the way Hans had to pass Egeskov Manor which
lay quite near to his mother's house. As he sped through
the gates the Lord of the Manor's only daughter, who
was standing at the window, burst out laughing at the
sight of the sleigh. Hans thought she was making fun of
him and became very angry. He made his second wish,
muttering, 'Yes, you may laugh at me now, young lady,
but before a year has passed you will have something
very different to think about.'

Hans now drove on and neither he nor the Lord of
the Manor's daughter thought any more of this incident.
Within a year, however, the Lord's daughter had a son,
and no one knew who the father was. The Lord of the
Manor was furious. If only the father had been a duke
or a baron, he thought, then it wouldn't matter so much.
When the little boy was three years old, and as no one

had turned up to claim him, the Lord decided that it was time his grandson had a father. So he spread the news far and wide that he was looking for a father for his daughter's child and all young men, rich or poor, were to come to the manor on an appointed day. The little boy was to choose his father in this way: he would be holding an apple in his hand and the man he gave the apple to was to become his father and immediately marry his mother.

At last the day arrived, and young men from near and far came streaming up the manor drive in the hope, not so much of becoming the boy's father, but of marrying the Lord of the Manor's daughter. Some came simply out of curiosity – and one of these was Hans who had now grown up and was a handsome, hefty youth, but still as lazy as ever. However, that day his curiosity had proved stronger than his laziness, and so he idled along behind the others, for it was too much of an effort for him to keep up with them. By the time the other young men had entered the manor and had been introduced to the boy, Hans was still a long way off.

Inside the house the little boy looked in wonder at all these visitors, but he held his apple firmly and gave not the slightest indication of wanting to part with it. The Lord of the Manor was just becoming restless and annoyed when the door opened and in walked Hans. No sooner did the little boy see him than he ran across the room and gave Hans the apple. When he saw who was to be the boy's father, the Lord of the Manor's patience was exhausted. He shouted, he raved and he swore. He couldn't bear to think that his daughter would have to live with such a lazy lout and he never wanted to set eyes on her again. Thus, that same day, on the Lord's instructions his daughter and her little son and lazy Hans were taken away to an uninhabited island where they would have to fend for themselves as best they could.

There they were on a lonely island without food or shelter. The girl and her little son cried while Hans lay down and moped. At last the Lord's daughter asked Hans to tell her who he was and how he had spent his life; perhaps from this she might be able to find out what had brought them together. He told her his whole life-story, what a lazy boy he had been and about his errand to the sea-shore. He told her about the goldfish and his three wishes, about the sleigh and how she had laughed at him; and what had happened to her since then was the result of his second wish. Now she began to understand. 'But you still have one wish left, haven't you Hans? If so, we can put everything right.'

Hans certainly had one more wish left, and so she asked him to wish that she could have as many wishes fulfilled as there were tucks in her apron. He did as she asked and then she started wishing: a wonderful manor with the finest furniture, beautiful flower-gardens, fountains and lawns, white horses with flowing manes, and one splendid thing after another. And immediately, everything she wished for, she had. Most important of all, however, she wished that Hans, her future husband, would turn into a hardworking and reliable person instead of the lazy good-for-nothing he was now, and from that very moment Hans became the most helpful and industrious man you could imagine. Then he and his wife returned to the home of the Lord of the Manor, and told him how everything had come about. When he saw all their wealth and splendour, the Lord of the Manor was no longer angry and accepted both of them again. He now invited them to stay with him, but to this they said, 'No, thank you,' for they had a far more splendid home themselves. The Lord of the Manor often visited them and grew very fond of Hans; and I am sure that to this very day Hans, his wife and their son are all living happily together.

K

FOURTEEN

Three Pennyworth

THERE WAS ONCE a soldier who had served in King Christian's army for eight long years. Now the wars were over and he looked forward to going home once more. But all he received in payment for his service were three pennies. He was disappointed, but set out on his way with a good heart, determined to make the most of what he had. Along the road he went, swinging his stick and singing merrily; and his clear voice echoed in the hills. He had not gone far when he was stopped by an old woman who asked for a little money. 'All I have in the world are three pennies,' replied the soldier, 'but it doesn't matter much whether I have three or two, so you may as well have this penny.' The woman thanked him, put the coin in her pocket and went on. The soldier had not travelled more than a few miles when he met an old woman by the wayside – the same old woman as before, but he didn't notice it. 'Have you got a spare coin for an old woman?' she asked. 'I have only two pennies, but whether I have two or one, it doesn't much matter,' he replied, and gave her a second penny. 'May God bless you for your kindness!' she said, and continued on her journey. A few minutes later another woman greeted him, and he still didn't realize that it was the same one who had stopped him before. 'I suppose you haven't a coin for a poor old woman?' she asked. 'As a matter of fact I have exactly one left, so you may as well have it, for whether I have a penny or nothing I am equally poor.' The old woman took the coin and trundled off.

The soldier went on walking, his only possession being the old clothes he was wearing and the knapsack on his back, and that was light for it contained only a patched shirt and a pair of darned socks. And even if his pocket was light, too, so was his heart. He walked on swinging his stick, and his cheerful voice resounded in the hills. Eventually he came to a wood and here he met the old woman who had taken all his money. 'Good day, young man,' said the old woman, 'can you spare a few minutes to talk to me?' 'Of course, if it will please you,' answered the soldier, 'but what do you want to talk to me about?' 'I wonder whether you would like three wishes,' said the old woman. 'I certainly should,' replied the soldier. 'Make your three wishes then,' said the woman. And it didn't take the soldier long to decide. First he asked for God's grace and friendship; then he wished that his knapsack would never wear out; finally he wished that it would hold everything he wanted it to hold, and that what was already there would stay there until he wanted it out again. 'It shall be as you have wished,' said the old woman. 'Good-bye and good luck on your journey.' The soldier thanked her and on he went.

The soldier walked on whistling merrily and for the time being thought no more of the old woman, for she had probably been joking. After a few miles, however, he found his thoughts returning to the three wishes. If what the old woman had said was true, he mused, his three wishes might prove very useful. He had now come to the heath where lay heather, sand and stone after stone. By this time he was so lost in his thoughts that he stumbled against a huge stone. 'I wish you were in my

knapsack and out of my way!' he exclaimed. No sooner
had he uttered these words than the stone had disappeared. The soldier soon discovered where it was, however, for his knapsack felt as heavy as lead. He fell
backwards and quickly found himself standing on his
head. He was dazed and tried to work out what had
happened, and gradually it dawned on him that he was
in his present state because of the wish he had made. He
quickly wished the stone back on the ground again; and
just as quickly he somersaulted back on to his feet. From
now on, he decided, he would put his wishes to better
use.

Many a mile the soldier travelled that day, and as
evening approached he felt very hungry. He was passing
a manor and thought that here he might be able to beg
a sandwich, for without food he could not go much
farther. Up the path and round the back of the big
house he went. Then he knocked on the door and waited.
The servant who opened it was very busy cooking her
master's dinner. 'Can you spare a morsel of bread for a
poor soldier?' he asked, but the servant said that, much
as she would like to help him, the food was so carefully
rationed that not a crumb remained after every member
of the household had eaten. However, the Lord of the
Manor might give him both food and a little money to
help him on his way, and so she showed the soldier
where to find her master. He thanked her and walked
across the hallway to the Lord of the Manor's room.
He put his ear to the keyhole and listened. He heard the
tinkling of coins. Then he knocked nervously.

Meanwhile, inside, the Lord of the Manor was busily
counting his money. On the table in front of him stood
a big earthenware pot full of pure golden coins, and on
the floor beside him was a large wooden chest full of
shining silver shillings. The Lord was so engrossed in

what he was doing that the knock on the door startled him. But then he thought that it was probably only a peasant who had come to pay his tythes. This cheered him up and quite jovially he shouted, 'Come in!' When, however, he saw before him a soldier, begging for food, he soon changed his tune. In a violent temper the Lord of the Manor immediately ordered him outside, and it took the soldier no more than a few seconds to reach the highway again.

But he had kept his eyes open and hadn't left without noticing the earthenware pot full of golden coins and the wooden chest full of silver shillings. 'What a selfish man that Lord of the Manor is!' he thought to himself. 'I'll teach him a lesson. I'll make him sorry for treating me like this.' He then wished that the golden coins were in his knapsack. Swish! And they were all there. He would like the silver shillings, too, but he couldn't possibly carry them all, so he wished he had a quarter of them. Swish! And they were in his knapsack, exactly the number he had wanted. 'The Lord of the Manor has only himself to blame for losing his money,' said the soldier to himself as he continued his journey.

Towards evening he came to a small town and by now he felt famished. So he went to the biggest inn he could find and sat down to dinner. He ate his meal so quickly that the fine gentlemen sitting around the table started whispering about this simple fellow who gobbled up his food as though he hadn't eaten for a week. At last the gentlemen got up from the table and paid, but the soldier searched first in one pocket, then in another, pretending he couldn't find his money. Out of the corners of their eyes the others watched and tittered, and one of them remarked that although the soldier might have forgotten his money he certainly hadn't forgotten how to eat. Having turned out all his pockets, the soldier started rummaging in his knapsack. At this they burst out laughing, and the worried look on the innkeeper's face made them even more amused. When the soldier threw two golden coins on the table and told the innkeeper to keep the change, however, a sudden silence fell upon the room. The frown on the innkeeper's face quickly turned into a smile, and he bowed and thanked the rich stranger over and over again. He then asked whether the soldier would do him the honour of sharing a bottle of wine with him. The soldier, of course, didn't refuse, and when they had emptied the bottle he asked the innkeeper if he could find him a room for the night. The innkeeper apologized profusely for every room had been taken; that is, all except one which could not be used. Everyone who had slept in this room had met a violent death on the first night, and so far three people had died there. Since then the room had been locked up. This story didn't alarm the soldier, however, and he replied brightly, 'It will do for me. When it is ready I want you to lay supper for four, and set on the table four candles, four bottles of your best wine and four packs of cards. Then bring me the key to the room.' The innkeeper said that if this was what the stranger wanted he would obey and the room would be ready by bed-time, but he walked off with a look of fear and bewilderment on his face.

Evening came. The soldier went up to his bedroom and saw that everything was nicely laid just as he had asked. There on the table were four candles, four bottles of wine and four packs of cards. He emptied the gold and silver coins from his knapsack and lit the candles. Then he sat quite still, waiting for whatever might turn up. Not many minutes passed before he heard a great noise in the chimney and a big black lump rolled out of the stove and on to the floor where it unfurled itself.

Before him stood a long black troll, with horns and tail and with claws and fangs. Although it looked hideous, the soldier did not panic. Instead, he said politely, 'Sit down, my good friend, and help yourself.' Hardly had he said this when another noise followed by yet another came from the chimney, and each time a black lump came rolling out of the stove. A second, then a third black troll each uglier than the one before, unfurled themselves. But the soldier received them all with equal calmness and with equal kindness. He asked them to sit down and take pot luck. So they all sat down, ate a hearty meal and drank good wine. When the table had been cleared they started playing cards, each with his own pack, but at the same time the trolls moved nearer and nearer the soldier until they were no more than an arm's length away. Then they started tugging at him.

'You're getting too close for my liking,' murmured the soldier, beginning to feel uncomfortable. 'I wish you were all in my knapsack.' Swish! In they went. And however much they wriggled and writhed they couldn't escape. 'Listen,' ordered the soldier, 'you may as well settle down because you can't get out and, besides, I want to talk to you.' At this they became quiet and the soldier went on, 'Now tell me why you come here whenever anyone sleeps in this room!' They told him that under the stove was a big kettle full of money. 'Is that the only reason?' remarked the soldier. 'Still, we'll leave it like that for the time being. I'm tired now and must rest. Good night and sleep tight.' With that he undressed and went to bed.

The soldier slept soundly until dawn when the innkeeper came up to his room. He stooped to look through the key-hole and saw the soldier lying quite still, but whether he was alive or dead he couldn't tell. He knocked, opened the door and went in, calling out to wake him up. Startled and very angry, the soldier sat up in bed and told the innkeeper off for waking him. He had paid well for his room, he said, and was entitled to peace and quiet night and morning. Although taken aback at this outburst, the innkeeper felt relieved that the soldier was alive and that the spooks had not caused him any harm. He inquired whether anything unusual had happened during the night, but the soldier insisted on finishing his sleep, so he just had to wait. It was late in the morning when the soldier got up and dressed, and hoping his guest was now in a better temper, the innkeeper asked again about the previous night. The only reply he received, however, was that the soldier had enjoyed a good night's sleep and was now ready for a good lunch. When he had eaten the soldier summoned the innkeeper and asked him to find the two strongest men in town. 'Certainly!' replied the innkeeper, anxious to please; 'but may I be so bold as to ask what you need them for?' he inquired timidly.

To satisfy the innkeeper's curiosity the soldier told him that he wanted the knapsack taken to the black-smith for a good beating, so dusty had it become on the highway. Two very strong men were necessary to carry it to the forge for it was so heavy. 'Two strong men to take the knapsack to the blacksmith to be beaten!' muttered the innkeeper. 'The poor chap is suffering from a hang-over. I thought he drank more than was good for him last night.' But the innkeeper would do anything for a lark, and so he promised to go at once to find the two strongest men in town. Not very long after-wards he returned, followed by two solid-looking fellows with rippling muscles. The soldier told them that if they would carry his knapsack to the forge for him he would give each of them a rigsort (old Danish coin the equiva-lent of sixpence). Never would they get the chance to earn such easy money again, thought the two fellows, and gladly accepted. They very soon discovered, however, that they would earn every penny of it, for the knapsack was so heavy that with every step they took they nearly sank to their knees. The way to the forge seemed endless. Finally, panting heavily, they arrived at the blacksmith's and dropped the knapsack. The inn-keeper, who had followed behind, went up to the smith and told him that a soldier had sent this knapsack to have all the dust beaten out of it. Noticing the puzzled look on the smith's face, he whispered that the soldier had been drinking heavily the night before and that this request was probably the outcome of it. Still, he was rich and a good customer, so they both might be well rewarded. Blacksmiths are usually jovial and this one was certainly no exception. With a wink at the inn-keeper he called his apprentices, thinking they might share in the fun, and this kind of work would undoubtedly be new to them. At this point the soldier entered the forge and asked the smith how much he would charge for doing this job for him. 'Two rigsort ought to cover it,' answered the smith. That surely wasn't enough, replied the soldier; in fact, if he could have the job done really well he would pay a whole rigsdaler (old Danish coin equal to a florin). 'I'll see to it you are satisfied,' promised the smith. 'When we have finished not a speck of dust will you find on the knap-sack but,' he added jokingly, 'it remains to be seen whether anything is left of your knapsack.' 'Don't worry about that!' said the soldier. Grunting and groaning, the two hefty fellows lifted the sack on to the anvil and the smith's three apprentices, having rolled up their sleeves and spat on their hands, began beating the dust off it. This was certainly the funniest job they had ever undertaken. Suddenly they stopped. From the knapsack

They hammered with all their might.

came a yelling and a squealing such as they had never heard before. Puzzled, they looked at the soldier, but he told them to take no notice and to get on with their work. Blow after blow they rained on the knapsack until sweat poured in torrents down their black faces. 'The knapsack can't last much longer,' they panted, and this thought spurred them on. But an hour later when they stopped to inspect the knapsack it showed not the slightest sign of wear.

'Yes, give it a good beating!' encouraged the soldier; 'that knapsack needs it for it has been collecting dust for donkey's years.' The three gay youths gradually grew tired of that game, however, and seeing that all their strength was spent, the blacksmith shouted for three more apprentices to carry on where the others had left off. These were strong and fresh, and even though the leather might be bewitched, they certainly knew what iron was like and decided to concentrate on smashing up the iron buckles on the knapsack. They hammered with all their might, but the iron was just as tough as the leather. At last they dropped their hammers, exhausted. That was enough, thought the soldier, and handed the smith the rigsdaler in payment. Then he asked the two strong fellows who had brought the knapsack to the forge to carry it to the stream on the outskirts of the town. There he opened the knapsack. Inside, brimful, he found a heap of black dust, all that remained of the trolls' bodies. He emptied the dust into the stream and walked back into the town with the innkeeper.

Back in his room, the soldier told the innkeeper that a kettle full of money was hidden in his house, and if they could share it equally, he would show him where to find it. To this the innkeeper gladly agreed, and the stove in the soldier's bedroom was broken up. Sure enough, there underneath it was the big kettle full to the brim with money. The innkeeper was so pleased that he gave the soldier several acres of his own land which lay outside the town. There the soldier built a house of his own and lived happily and comfortably for many years. He enjoyed God's grace and favour and everything he wanted he could have – yes, a Danish soldier received all this in exchange for three pennies.

FIFTEEN

The Loveliest Rose

THERE ONCE LIVED a merchant who had three daughters. The two eldest were ugly and vain, but the youngest was both beautiful and kind. One spring the merchant had to make a long journey across the sea to buy his wares. On the eve of his departure he called his daughters to his room and asked what presents they would like him to bring home for them. It did not take them long to make up their minds. The eldest daughter decided upon a fine dress, the other wanted a new hat, while the youngest, whose name was Marie, asked her father to bring home the loveliest rose he could find.

The merchant took leave of his children and sailed far away to a large and wonderful city. Here in the early morning he anchored his ship and went up into the market-place where he made some good bargains. In the late afternoon, having completed his dealings, he remembered his daughters' wishes and at once went into a shop where he bought the finest dress and most beautiful hat he could find; but not a single rose did he see. He searched from one end of the city to the other, but all in vain. Finally, he bought some trinkets which he would give to his youngest daughter instead. But when on the following day he wanted to return home, his ship would not move in spite of the strong wind that was blowing. Thus he lowered all the sails and went back up to the city, convinced that his boat would not move off because he had failed to keep his promise to his youngest daughter. This time he walked outside the city gates and eventually he came to a magnificent castle. In front of the castle was a beautiful garden and in the middle of the garden grew a rose-tree on which bloomed the loveliest rose he had ever seen.

The merchant looked around him and, as nobody was in sight, he tiptoed into the garden and plucked the rose. He had just taken the rose when a handsome prince appeared before him and stormed, 'How dare you steal my rose?' The merchant lowered his head in shame and begged forgiveness. He told the prince about his daughters and of the promise he had made to the youngest. The prince, no longer angry, listened intently to his story and then invited the merchant into his castle. From a drawer in his desk he took out a picture of a very beautiful woman and asked whether the merchant thought his daughter was as beautiful as she. The merchant was amazed, for there before him was a portrait of his youngest daughter. 'But this is my own child, my own little Marie!' he exclaimed. The prince was equally surprised and told him that one night many weeks ago he had dreamt of a very beautiful woman whom he had taken for his bride. As soon as he had awoken he had drawn a picture of her, and now he realized his dream must be fulfilled. He allowed the merchant to keep the stolen rose and bade him also take a mirror and a letter home to Marie.

The merchant thus hurried back to his ship, and when he had weighed anchor, a fresh wind immediately filled the sails. After a few days he reached home, safe and well, and was received with great joy, especially by his children, each of whom had long looked forward to the expected present. The two eldest were delighted with the hat and the dress, but Marie remained silent when she was given, not only the loveliest rose anyone had ever seen, but also a sweet little letter and a beautiful mirror. She hurried upstairs into her room, closed the door and with her heart pounding, opened the letter.

That very moment a little bird fluttered outside the window.

How excited and happy she was to discover that it was a prince who loved her and whom she could see when she looked in the mirror and spoke his name three times!

As soon as she had read the letter she took the mirror and very softly called the prince's name three times. That very moment a little bird fluttered outside the window and pecked on the window-pane with its beak as if asking permission to come in. At once Marie opened the window, and when the bird flew in, there, immediately in front of her, stood a handsome prince. He told her about his dream and about his love for her; and before he flew away again he gave her a huge nut which he asked her to open after he had gone. When shortly afterwards Marie opened the nut there unfolded before her a dress of the finest silk, as blue as the sea and sparkling with the rarest gems. Her two vain sisters gasped in wonder as Marie came down in her wonderful dress.

Marie hardly slept that night, and the next day was not very old before the longing for her dear prince became so strong that she went up to her room, took the mirror, opened the window and called him three times. The sisters, who sensed something was brewing, tiptoed silently after her, peeped through a crack in the door and listened. When Marie came down she had on a new silk dress even lovelier than the previous one, and the sisters became so envious of her that they plotted to ruin her happiness.

Next day they persuaded Marie, who was always kind and helpful, to go to town on an errand. No sooner was she gone than they ran up to her room, took the mirror, opened the window and shouted the name of the prince three times. The bird came immediately, and when it was well inside the room they closed the window in order to prevent it from escaping. Realizing that it had been tricked, the bird flew so hard against the window that the glass broke; and as it flew out it cut its breast so deeply that the blood ran down the pane.

When Marie came back and went up to her room to call her prince, she noticed feathers and blood on the broken pane and a strange fear seized her. She quickly caught hold of the mirror, but however often she called her betrothed he did not appear.

Overcome by grief, she ran away from her home and out into the world to seek the prince. Days and nights she walked until late one evening she came to a great forest in which she lost her way. Tired and disheartened, she threw herself to the ground, weeping and shouting for help. Suddenly, deep in the forest, she saw a light. She got up and walked towards it. At length she reached a cottage and inside found an old woman whom she asked to help her in her distress. After listening carefully to all that Marie told her, the old woman bade her set a kettle on the fire and, when it was boiled, she was to drop her lovely rose into the water. It saddened her to lose her lovely rose, but if she could find and save her prince no sacrifice was too dear. When at last the rose had been boiled the old woman took a bottle and poured the water into it. She then gave Marie a hat, a coat and a pair of trousers which she asked her to put on. Her prince, she told her, was dying and, so far, no doctor had been able to save him although the King had promised half his kingdom to the one who could do so. Now all Marie had to do was to take the bottle with the water and, as soon as it was daylight, go up to the castle, which stood at the edge of the forest, and pretend to be a doctor who had come from a foreign country to save the prince. As soon as she was inside with the sick prince she was to bathe his chest with the water which she had in the bottle and everything would turn out well for both of them.

Marie thanked the old woman who had been so kind to her and early the next morning she put on the new clothes and set off. She had just reached the edge of the forest when she caught sight of a great and wonderful

L

castle which was surrounded by a beautiful garden. Outside the gate stood a sentry who barred her way; but when she said she was a doctor who had come from a foreign country to save the sick prince, the news was brought to the King's notice and immediately she was allowed inside.

The castle was as still as the grave, and when she entered the prince's room there he lay with his eyes closed, his face as pale as death. Several doctors stood at the bedside and said that now there was no more hope of saving him. Then, walking up to the bed, Marie poured a few drops from her bottle on to the dying prince and at once he opened his eyes. A few minutes later she emptied half the contents of the bottle on to his chest and then he started to stir; but when she had bathed him for the third time the wound healed and blood again flowed through his veins. He now got up, and when he fixed his gaze on the young doctor, Marie let fall the clothes the old woman had given her. 'Marie!' exclaimed the prince. She, too, called out his name, and they both flung their arms around each other's neck with joy and happiness, to the great amazement of both the King and everyone who looked on.

The prince and Marie now told them the whole story, and when the King heard it he gladly consented to the prince's marriage to Marie who had already won the right to half his kingdom. The wedding was celebrated with great rejoicing, and they lived happily together all their days.

SIXTEEN

The Fox and the Stork

ONCE UPON A time two neighbours of the forest, the fox and the stork, decided to pool all their food; and to save each other work they came to an arrangement whereby they took it in turn to do the cooking. Unfortunately, when they served the food the fox used a pan and the stork a pot; and they grumbled and groaned as they tried to eat, for the fox could get nothing out of the pot and the stork fared almost as badly with the pan. As the days went by their frayed tempers reached boiling-point until finally their friendship ended and war was declared. What a commotion the news caused in the surrounding countryside! Everyone was eager to see the battle and wondered who would win.

The appointed day came. Tingling with excitement, men, women and children from near and far made their way to the scene of the contest. But on a near-by farm the poor maid was left all alone to look after the house. She was bitterly disappointed and as the day wore on she became more and more lonely and bored. 'I should love to go,' she thought, 'not just for the battle but to see all the people who are watching. If I were to fasten all the windows, lock all the doors and take the keys with me there's no reason why I shouldn't go. And if I come home a little before the others and put everything neat and tidy, nobody will know the difference for there will be nothing to grumble about.' Her mind was made up. She shut the windows, locked the doors and, with the keys in her pocket, dashed down the path in the direction of the battlefield. Soon she came to the big stream and had to pull up sharply as the plank had been washed away by the torrent. The stream was too wide for her to jump across so she just stood on the bank, panting and perspiring and wondering what to do. Meanwhile she took a handkerchief from her pocket to mop the sweat from her brow. Unfortunately, the keys got tangled up with her handkerchief and dropped into the water. She burst out crying and was very unhappy. Her master and mistress would rant and rave at her and tell her to leave when they came home and found themselves locked out; and she certainly wouldn't find another job.

As she stood there moping, her eyes wet with tears, a mountain-man came up to her. 'Why are you so sad, little girl?' he inquired. When she had poured out her story he said he would help her, not only to recover the lost keys, but also to cross the water if, in return, she would promise to give him in ten years' time either her first-born son or a sack of gold. She was so distressed that she made her promise at once and the mountain-man carried her across the stream, but the keys he said he would keep until she came back.

At last she reached the battlefield, but the thought of the mountain-man and the keys preyed on her mind so much that she hardly realized what she was watching. It was no use, she couldn't enjoy herself; so she quietly slipped off home well before the end of the fight.

There by the stream the mountain-man was waiting to help her across the water and to give her the farmhouse keys. She arrived home with plenty of time to spare, and by the time her master and mistress returned, a meal was laid on the table and everything was spick and span. They never dreamt that their maid had been out and, of course, knew nothing of her promise to the mountain-man.

Shortly afterwards the maid married a farmer's son and from her very first day in her new home she started saving. She looked twice at every skilling (penny) before she spent it and put aside nearly everything her husband gave her. This naturally pleased her old mother-in-law although she wasn't to know that the money was intended for the mountain-man. But a sack of gold isn't easy to fill, and when a year after her marriage the girl had a son, she realized that if the mountain-man wasn't to have him she must hurry up and fill the sack with gold.

Her son grew up into a lively little boy and often wondered why his mother hid all the gold in the cellar. He frequently asked her, but never received a straightforward answer until his tenth year. His mother could now hide her secret no longer for she had only saved a few thousand rigsdaler (florins), and the sack was still only half full. With tears in her eyes she told him of her promise to the mountain-man, but when the little boy had heard her story he put on a brave face and said, 'Don't worry any more about the gold, mother. I'm not in the least bit afraid of the mountain-man. Now, stop crying and cheer up.'

On the boy's tenth birthday there came a loud knock on the farm-house door. It was, as they expected, the mountain-man. The boy's mother wrung her hands in despair, but there was not a thing she could do. She had made a bargain and she must keep to it. On the other hand the boy remained calm and composed and said, 'I'm so glad you've come as I've always wanted to see where you live.' The mountain-man needed no second asking; he grabbed the boy by a leg and an arm, swung him over his shoulder and trotted off.

A few months later the mountain-man had to go on a journey and before he set out he told the boy what to do; he was to clean the stables thoroughly and if he hadn't finished by when the mountain-man came home, woe betide him. 'Then I shall kill you,' threatened the mountain-man; 'and remember not to go behind the barn under the big lime-tree, for if you do I'll chop your head off.'

When the mountain-man had gone the boy set to work, but as the floors and walls were thickly plastered with dirt his task was no easy one. It soon dawned on him that to finish before the mountain-man came home was completely out of the question. That the mountain-man would kill him was certain, and so, thinking that he might as well be hanged for a sheep as a lamb, he decided to find out what secret lay behind the barn, for after all he could only have his head cut off once. Thus he went round to the back of the barn and was surprised to see a beautiful maiden who sat spinning cotton, and lying beside her were three dogs and a grey calf.

'The mountain-man will kill you if he finds you here,' she cried. 'You must not stay another second.' 'I'm well aware of that,' replied the boy, 'but I shall lose my life anyway because I shan't have finished cleaning the stables out before he comes home, and so I thought I might as well have a good look round before I die. I'm so glad I came and found another human being like myself.' 'Listen to me!' said the girl. 'If you will be faithful to me I will do my best to help you.' The boy gladly promised and the girl at once gave her orders. 'Clean!' she shouted to the one dog. 'Sweep up!' she said to the second. 'Sprinkle sand!' she commanded the third. The dogs immediately set to work and in the space of a few seconds the whole stable was clean and tidy. The boy was amazed. 'Be sure not to mention that you've been to see me,' warned the maiden, 'otherwise we shall both suffer.'

The mountain-man returned the following day and, having found everything to his satisfaction, lay down and slept, for he had been on a long journey and was very weary.

The next morning he had to go out again and before leaving he said to the boy, 'I shall be away again today, so listen to what you have to do. This horn here is full of malt and this thimble is full of hops, and from that I want you to brew some beer so strong that it will put even a mountain-man to sleep. You had better finish by the time I come home or I'll tear you apart. And don't forget what I said about going to the barn!'

As soon as the mountain-man had disappeared the boy ran straight to the maiden and poured out his troubles. She did her best to console him and said that if he would be faithful to her she would help him. She then shouted to the first dog, 'Brew beer!' To the second she said, 'Add yeast!' And the third she commanded, 'Stir well!'

The work was soon done and the boy was happy again. But the maiden warned him that their troubles were not yet over. That night when the mountain-man was fast asleep – and the boy would be able to tell that because his eyes would be as big as mill-wheels – he was to hurry round to her and then they would escape together; for the mountain-man would eventually either cut off his head or ask him to perform tasks that even she could not manage.

The mountain-man came home in the evening and found everything to his satisfaction. He still went round to the maiden, however, and told her to cut off the boy's

Then she was to make a big fire under the furnace . . .

head as soon as he had fallen asleep. Then she was to make a big fire under the furnace and boil his body in order to make him tender.

When the mountain-man started to snore the maiden lit the fire, pricked her finger and let three drops of blood fall into the furnace. She hastily fetched the boy and the grey calf, and the three of them made off as fast as their legs would carry them.

It was dawn when the mountain-man awoke and shouted, 'Is that boy boiled yet?' 'No, I've only just started boiling him,' replied the first drop of blood. The mountain-man thought it was the girl who answered him and settled down to sleep again. Some time later he cried out again, 'Surely he's boiled by now'; but the second drop of blood replied, 'No, he is only half-boiled.' The mountain-man rolled over on to his other side and was soon snoring again. Shortly afterwards he awoke again and shouted, 'Is he ready now?' And to his great satisfaction the third drop of blood answered, 'Yes.'

Bleary-eyed, the mountain-man jumped out of bed, ran up to the furnace and reached for his big meat-fork which was hanging on the wall. He dug it into the furnace and, without looking what he was doing, put the first thing he caught hold of into his mouth. He chewed and chewed until he began to feel sick. Then he spat out his 'food', and when he saw a pair of old leather boots he was livid with anger. He raged and he swore and his old manservant came in to inquire what was the matter. 'Quickly,' he screamed, 'run after the maiden who has fled with the boy and bring them back here so that I can kill them.' The manservant raced off in the direction they had taken.

When they had been travelling for some time, the maiden said to the boy, 'Turn round and see whether anyone is following us.' 'There seems to be an awful lot of steam,' the boy replied. 'That must be the mountain-man's servant coming after us,' concluded the maiden. 'Listen! pluck one hair from my head and one from yours; then throw yours to the right and mine to the left and wish that I may become a tree and you a bird singing away in the branches.' The boy did as she bade him and at once his wish was fulfilled.

Eventually the manservant arrived there and, seeing only a tree with a bird singing in the branches, he turned about and ran back home. When he reported what he had seen the mountain-man became even angrier. 'You fool!' he cried. 'Go straight back to the same place and uproot everything you catch sight of.' Anxious to pacify his master, the manservant hurried off the way he had just come.

When they had travelled a few more miles the maiden asked the boy to see whether anyone was coming after them. 'He's coming after us again,' said the boy fearfully. 'Quick! throw one of your hairs to the right and one of mine to the left! Wish that I may become a church and that you may become a parson preaching the sermon!' the maiden commanded. The boy did as he was told and immediately the wish was fulfilled.

At last the manservant arrived at that place and, seeing only the church with the parson preaching the sermon inside, he went back home. 'You silly fool!' cried the mountain-man when he heard his story. 'I can see I shall have to go myself'; and off he went as fast as he could.

They had gone a good distance when the maiden asked the boy if anyone was following them. 'Yes,' he replied, 'whatever shall we do this time?' 'Take one of my hairs and one of yours, throw them to either side and wish that I may become a lake and you a duck swimming about on it.'

The mountain-man at last reached them and when he saw the duck swimming on the lake, he was furious. He flung himself to the ground in his temper and decided to drink up the lake. This proved too hard for him, however, and before he realized it he had burst and become a flint-stone; and from then on he never harmed anyone again.

The maiden and the boy hurried along until they came to a very beautiful forest. They wandered down one of the paths and at last reached a cottage. They looked inside but found it quite empty, so they decided to rest after their long journey. The next morning the boy said to the maiden, 'Today I am going to my parents' home for a cart to fetch you in. Now stay here and don't wander away while I am gone.' 'Very well,' replied the maiden, 'but you will also need to take care, for on the edge of the forest you will pass a manor. You must promise me not to go in there for, if you do, you will soon forget me.' The boy made his promise and off he went.

As the boy passed the manor the sound of music and laughter reached his ears. He stood for a few minutes and listened. Then a couple of jovial fellows came out and invited him inside. The boy remembered the maiden's warning and would not be tempted; but the two young men wouldn't take 'no' for an answer and, putting their arms around his shoulders, they dragged him into the manor. Soon afterwards a girl came up to him and asked him to dance. She was so pretty that he couldn't refuse and together they danced and sang; and in all the noise and gaiety he forgot his promise to the maiden.

Meanwhile, the maiden was sitting in her forest cottage longing for the boy's return. A servant of the Lord of the Manor happened to be passing one day and,

wondering who could be living there, he opened the
door and went inside. When he saw the beautiful maiden
who lived there, he became quite enamoured with her
and stayed there until dark. The maiden soon grew
tired of his advances and said, 'I'm afraid I have forgotten to close the door.' 'Let me close it for you,' the
servant immediately volunteered. 'Thank you! Just let
me know when you have caught hold of the handle,'
said the maiden. The servant went to the door and
grasped the handle, shouting, 'I have it now.' 'Good!'
exclaimed the maiden. 'You've got hold of it, and it has
got hold of you. And I hope the door will bang open
and shut all night long.' The door certainly did bang
open and shut all night long and the poor servant was
dragged backwards and forwards with it. The sweat
poured off him in buckets and it wasn't until dawn that
he was able to free himself. He was so anxious to escape
that he ran off home like a scalded cat without even
saying good-bye to the maiden. Nor, of course, did he
tell anybody else of his misfortune.

A few days later the Lord of the Manor's coachman
called at the cottage. He, too, wanted to woo the maiden
and he, too, stayed with her until late in the evening. At
last the maiden said that she must poke the fire. 'No,
I'll do that for you,' offered the coachman, eager to
please. But when he caught hold of the poker the
maiden said, 'Now you have hold of it, and it has hold of
you; and you must poke the fire until tomorrow morning.' By the time morning came the coachman was
sweating like a bull and was covered all over in ashes.
He was jolly glad when he found that he could free himself, and, letting go of the poker, he ran out of the house
as fast as his legs could carry him. He had had enough
of love.

One day the Lord of the Manor's bailiff decided to

visit the cottage, and when he saw the face of the beautiful maiden at the window, he immediately went up to the door and knocked. The maiden let him in and the bailiff became so infatuated with her that he made up his mind to stay until evening. But the maiden grew tired of his company and all the time she planned to get rid of him. At last she had an idea and cried out suddenly, 'Oh dear! my poor grey calf is out in the wood. I shall have to bring it in.' The bailiff immediately jumped to his feet and offered to go instead for, in this way, he might win her favour . 'It is no easy task,' warned the maiden, 'for the calf can only be guided in by its tail, and when you have caught hold of it you must call me.' Presently the bailiff shouted, 'I've got hold of its tail.' 'Well done!' exclaimed the maiden. 'You've got hold of it and it has got hold of you. And you can run after the calf over hill and dale until tomorrow morning.' Hardly had she said these words when the grey calf dashed off with the bailiff hanging on to its tail. Over hill and dale they went, all through the night until dawn when the bailiff managed to free himself. He certainly wouldn't ever visit the maiden in the cottage again and hobbled off home.

The years passed and the boy at the manor had now become a young man. He became friendly with one of the servant girls and after a few months they decided to get married. At last the wedding day came and they climbed up on to the coach for the ride to church. They had just sat down, however, when their seat cracked and finally broke. The other servants chased around but they could find nothing strong enough to bear the young couple's weight. Then the manservant who had been to the maiden's cottage remembered the front door. 'The very thing,' he cried. 'I'm sure it's strong enough'; and he proceeded to tell the others where the door could be found. This seemed a strange idea to the others but they would try anything to help the bridal pair out of their plight. They hurried off into the forest and brought back the door, but when they reached the manor gate the spike that holds the shafts snapped and no other could be found that was strong enough. Then the coachman, remembering the evening he had spent at the cottage, said, 'The maiden in the forest has a poker as well, and it's certainly a very strong one. Why don't we borrow that and use it as a spike?'

A young boy was sent off into the forest and the maiden gladly lent him her poker. Back he ran as quickly as he could and it was fitted on to the coach. Worse luck followed, however. Now the horses couldn't pull the coach. It was indeed an unlucky day and they had nearly decided to call a halt to the wedding when the bailiff exclaimed, 'I know. The maiden who lent us her front door and the poker has a grey calf. It's as strong as an ox and will pull the coach easily. Why don't we borrow that?' Everyone remarked that it would look very strange for a calf to draw the coach, but if it would help the bride and bridegroom out of their trouble that was all that mattered. Out to the maiden they ran for the third time and asked her whether they might borrow her grey calf. She agreed, but only on condition that she could come to the wedding herself. Of course, she could come, they said, and back they went with the calf. This time there was no further mishap, and with the old grey calf in front the coach drove off to church.

It so happened that at the celebration which followed, the married couple sat facing the maiden from the forest. When she had been sitting for a little while the maiden took two grains of corn and put them on the plate in front of her. She then caught hold of the two pigeons which were in her basket and placed them on the edge of the table. Seeing the grains of corn, the birds ran after them, but no matter how quickly they strutted backwards and forwards they didn't succeed in picking them up. 'They're certainly in a hurry,' laughed the bridegroom, watching the pigeons intently. 'Yes, you, too, were once in a hurry when you and I escaped from the mountain-man's home,' she replied. Suddenly he remembered her: it was the maiden he had left behind in the forest. He had broken his promise and had been so unfaithful to her, and he begged her forgiveness. She agreed to do so, but only if he left his bride and married her. Nothing would please him more, and so everybody visited the church for the second time to celebrate the wedding of the young man to his rightful betrothed.

And all this took place because the fox and the stork had declared war on each other.

SEVENTEEN

The Stupid Boy

THERE ONCE LIVED a woman who had a stupid son. One day, having watched his mother make butter in the dairy, he asked if he might go to town and sell it. 'Certainly not! You've never even been to town before!' exclaimed his mother. He kept on pestering, however, until eventually, in order to get rid of him, she gave him a lump of butter and told him to sell it as best he could.

The stupid boy then ambled off, and at length came to a huge stone. Believing the stone to be the town, he asked, 'Do you want to buy some butter?' There was, of course, no reply. 'Yes,' continued the boy, 'it's very fine butter I have. Here you are, have a little to taste.' So saying, he rubbed a pat of butter into the stone; and as it was a very hot day the sun at once melted it. Thinking the stone (or the town as he considered it) had eaten the butter, the stupid boy said, 'I see you can at least take the trouble to eat my butter. I suppose you may as well have it all; and the money can wait until tomorrow.' After rubbing all the butter into the stone, the boy returned home. 'Well, how have you fared today?' inquired his mother. 'I've sold all the butter to the town and will collect the money tomorrow,' replied the boy. 'What are you saying, you've sold the butter to the town?' cried his mother. 'Yes,' he answered. 'That's a fine tale, but who has bought it?' she demanded. 'I did as you said, mother, and sold the butter to the town,' replied the lad. 'Well,' she sighed, 'we've seen the last of that butter now. I ought to have had more sense than to have let you go off with it.'

Next day the boy wanted to go and fetch the money. It was no use his mother's saying he wouldn't get anything for it: he knew the town would pay. So he walked up to the stone and asked, 'May I have the money for the butter I sold you yesterday, good town?' As you would expect, the stone didn't answer. This made the boy quite cross and he began to scold the stone. 'You wretched town,' he cried, 'yesterday you bought butter from me and now you won't pay or even answer me. I'll jolly well show you that you're not dealing with a fool.' So saying, he caught hold of the stone and rolled it over.

Now under the stone lay a pot full to the brim with money. Very pleased with himself, he stuffed the coins into his pocket and set off home. When he put the money on the table his mother opened her eyes wide in amazement. 'Where on earth did you get all that from?' she asked. 'The town wouldn't pay or answer, so I got cross with him. I turned him over and took all the money from under him. I knew he had plenty of money but that he didn't want to part with it,' replied the boy. 'That's foolish,' cried his mother. 'You turned the town over? I should like to have seen that. But never mind, you've brought home a lot of money, and that's all that matters.'

Some months later it happened that the woman had to kill an animal. Her son again wanted to help her and volunteered to sell the meat. Remembering the boy's previous experience, she cut him a juicy steak and put

M

it in a basket. The boy set off and did not stop until he had reached the centre of the town. Here some dogs ran up to him, barking excitedly. 'Hullo! do you want to buy some meat?' he asked. The dogs barked in reply. 'All right, you may have a little to try,' went on the boy, throwing them a piece. The dogs soon ate it up, so he threw them all that remained in his basket. 'I'll come back and fetch the money tomorrow,' he said, and home he went.

Next day the stupid boy returned to the town, and there in the main street he met the dogs and bade them good day. 'May I have the money for the meat you had yesterday?' he asked. In reply they barked and barked but, of course, they gave him no money. 'So you don't want to pay,' he shouted angrily; 'I'll teach you a lesson, you hounds.' Now among the dogs was a little one with a pretty collar around its neck. Thinking this was the finest, he chased it along the street and into the parlour of a large house. Here he cornered it, grabbed it and tucked it under his arm, crying, 'So you won't pay eh! I'll teach you, believe me.' Then off the boy went to the King to complain about him and all the other dogs. Now the King had a beautiful daughter, but she was always so sad that he promised that anyone who succeeded in making her laugh could marry her and become ruler over his country. Up to the palace gates ambled the stupid boy with the little dog under his arm. The sentry, however, refused to allow him inside. 'Why can't I exercise my right to see the King when scoundrels cheat me?' demanded the boy. 'What do you want?' asked the soldier. 'I want to force the dog to pay for my meat,' replied the boy. 'Right, if you'll give me half of what you get for the meat, I'll let you inside,' said the sentry. The boy agreed; but inside the courtyard he encountered another sentry who stopped him and made him promise a quarter of what he received for the meat. On he went only to meet a third sentry who likewise made him promise a quarter of the price of the meat.

Without further hindrance the boy reached the King to whom he told his story. 'Well, if you are foolish enough to sell meat to dogs I can't help you. You must get the money from them yourself,' said the King impatiently. 'May the devil take possession of you, hound!' shouted the boy, taking the little dog by the collar and shaking him violently. Now at this, the King's daughter, who sat listening to everything in an adjoining room, could contain herself no longer and burst out laughing. The King was delighted. 'Now you can have plenty of money for your meat,' he cried, 'for now you may marry my daughter.' 'But I don't want her,' replied the boy. 'What, you don't want my daughter!' replied the King, surprised. 'Well, you may have a lump sum instead as I should really prefer you not to have her.' 'I don't want money either,' said the boy. 'If you don't want money, what do you want?' asked the King, growing more and more annoyed. 'I want sixty good strokes of the whip for my meat,' answered the boy. 'Very well,' agreed the King, 'but that is poor payment.' Then he summoned one of his courtiers and ordered him to mete out sixty strokes to the boy. 'Stop, stop!' shouted the boy. 'Those are for the sentries. The first shall have half the strokes, and the other two a quarter each, as I promised them payment for the meat.' And so the three sentries all had a good beating, each according to his due. 'You're not so stupid as you pretend,' said the King, adding, 'now I suppose you would like my daughter.' 'Yes,' replied the boy, 'I want her now because the sentries can't demand any more then they've got.' The stupid boy thus married the princess and they live a grand life to this very day.

I think the stupid boy did very well for himself, don't you?

EIGHTEEN

Peder Okse

ONCE UPON A time there lived a farmer and his wife. They owned a good farm and became very rich, but in spite of all their wealth they were unhappy, for they had no heir to inherit their money and property when they died. Now it happened one year that the man reared a pretty little bull and the couple decided to call it Peder. It was the loveliest animal they had ever seen; in fact it was so handsome and clever that it understood all that was said to it, and it was so gentle and playful that they looked after it as though it were their own child. As the months went by the farmer and his wife became more and more attached to the little bull. One day the man said to his wife, 'Do you think our churchsinger* could teach Peder to speak? If he could, then we should be able to adopt him as our own child so that he could inherit all we own.' 'I don't really know,' replied the woman, 'but our churchsinger is certainly very clever and he knows quite a lot more than the Lord's prayer. He might even be able to teach our Peder to talk. Why don't you go along and see him; there's no harm in trying?'

So off went the man to the churchsinger to ask him

* The churchsinger is a Danish church official who leads the congregational singing and says the opening and closing prayers. He wears a black suit.

whether he thought he could teach the bull to speak, so that it could inherit the farm after him. Now the church-singer was not only clever; he was cunning, too. He looked around to make sure nobody was listening; then in a low voice he said, 'Yes, I shall probably be able to teach your bull to speak, but not a word must you say to anyone, do you understand? It must all be done in secret, for if the Vicar hears he will be angry and will

He took the bull to the churchsinger, who promised to do his best

forbid me to do it. Now if I'm to do my best for Peder it will, of course, cost a lot of money, as I shall need the very best and most expensive books that can be bought.' 'The cost doesn't matter,' said the farmer. 'All we want is our Peder to talk. Here, for a start, is ten pounds to pay for the books.' So saying, he handed the church-singer the money, and promised on his honour not to breathe a word to anyone except his wife.

The same evening when darkness had fallen, he took the little bull to the churchsinger who promised to do his best. A week later, impatient to hear how Peder was getting on, the farmer called on the churchsinger again, but the latter advised him not to see the bull for the animal would grieve for him so much when he had gone, that it would forget everything it had learnt. However, to console the farmer for not being able to see his dear bull, the churchsinger told him that Peder was making good progress with his learning, but that he needed another ten pounds for some more books. Luckily the man had some money in his pocket, and having given it to the churchsinger, he went off home with high hopes.

Another week passed and back went the farmer to the churchsinger to hear how much progress Peder had made. 'Yes,' said the churchsinger, 'he's doing very well.' 'I don't suppose he can say anything yet?' inquired the man. 'Oh, yes,' replied the churchsinger, 'he can say "mea".' 'Poor soul,' said the man, 'he's trying to say mead. He probably wants some to drink. I'll go and buy him a barrel.' 'A good idea!' exclaimed the churchsinger. 'The mead will do Peder good.' So off went the farmer, and later the same day he returned with a barrel full of the best mead he could buy. Of course, as soon as he was gone the churchsinger drank it himself and gave the bull some milk for, after all, he thought, that would be better for him.

A week later the farmer returned to the churchsinger's house, wanting to hear what Peder could say now. 'I'm afraid he still keeps on saying "mea",' said the churchsinger. 'I think he is pulling our leg,' said the man, smiling to himself. 'Still, if he wants more mead, he shall certainly have it. But how is he getting on, otherwise?' 'Well, to tell the truth, I really need some more books,' answered the churchsinger. 'He doesn't seem to be learning much from the books he has at present.' 'Very well! If more books are needed, Peder shall have them,' said the man, and the same day he brought ten pounds for the churchsinger and another barrel of mead for the bull.

Peder's lessons were now proving so costly that the farmer decided to wait a few weeks before inquiring again about the bull's progress. After all it had cost him ten pounds every time he had visited the churchsinger so far, and at that rate he would soon spend all his money. Meanwhile the bull had grown quite fat, and receiving no more money from the farmer, the churchsinger had it killed. And many a fine meal the beast made him! Now the churchsinger was a crafty man and one evening he put on his black clothes and went to see the farmer. As soon as he had greeted the man and his wife, he said, 'I suppose Peder has come back here, hasn't he?' 'No, he hasn't,' replied the man anxiously. 'I do hope he hasn't run away.' 'I certainly hope not either,' said the churchsinger, 'he surely couldn't be so wicked and ungrateful as to do that, after all the hours and hours of teaching I've given him and after all the money I've spent on him myself – yes, I've paid at least ten pounds of my own money on books for him. And Peder had made such good progress that he could now say almost anything. In fact, only this morning, he said he longed to see his parents again. Because he had worked so hard I decided to reward him by bringing him home myself as he might not be sure of the way on his own. I had just closed my front door when I realized I had forgotten my walking stick and went back inside to fetch it. But when I came out again Peder had run off on his own. Naturally I thought he couldn't wait for me and had gone home, so if he's not here I don't know where on earth he can be.' Hearing this, the man and his wife burst out crying, for now, after all the money they had spent on his learning and just when they were going to have some pleasure from him, Peder had deserted them. Worst of all, however, they still had no heir. The churchsinger consoled them as best he could. He, too, pretended to be very sad. It was a big disappointment to him to lose his pupil just when he would have won praise and honour. But perhaps, after all, Peder was just lost, and he said he would inquire of his whereabouts in church the following Sunday. So saying, the churchsinger bade the couple farewell and off he went to a tasty dinner of roast veal.

Now it happened one day that, as the churchsinger was looking through his papers, he read of a merchant by name of Peder Okse who had settled in a town some distance away. He immediately sat up and thought deeply for a few moments. Then, folding the paper carefully, he put it in his pocket and walked over to the farm where the couple lived. He read the paragraph to them and then added, 'I shouldn't be at all surprised if this merchant isn't your Peder, the bull.' 'I'm positive it is,' said the man. 'Who else could it be?' 'Yes, it's Peder, all right,' agreed his wife. 'You must set off at once, and be sure you take plenty of money with you, for if our Peder has become a merchant, he will probably have need of some.'

The following day, with a bag of money slung over his shoulder, some sandwiches in his pocket and a pipe in his mouth, the farmer set off for the town where the merchant lived. It was a long journey and he tramped all day and night. Early the next morning, as dawn was breaking, he arrived at the town, and it didn't take him long to find the right house and ask whether the merchant was at home. 'Yes,' replied his servant, 'but he hasn't got up yet, and I daren't waken him.' 'Oh, don't worry about that,' said the farmer, pushing past him. 'I'm his father. Just show me up to his room!' The servant, thinking it would please his master, at once showed him the way to Peder's bedroom. Opening the door, the farmer looked inside the room, and there in bed lay the merchant, alone, for he was not yet married. The farmer recognized him at once. Yes, this was Peder all right, for he had exactly the same features as his own bull – a broad brow, a fat neck and red hair, but otherwise he looked just like any other human being. He went straight up to Peder and threw his arms around him. 'Oh, Peder!' he cried, 'I wish you knew how much your mother and I have been worrying about you since you ran away just after we had spent such a lot of money on your education. Now, on your feet, and let me have a good look at you!'

As you would expect, the merchant thought that the farmer was quite out of his mind, but since he might be dangerous it was best to take matters calmly. 'It won't take me more than a few moments to be ready,' he said, and hurriedly changed into his clothes. As Peder dressed, the farmer looked him up and down, saying, 'Our churchsinger is certainly a very brainy fellow for he has made a real man of you and has given you manners and breeding. Why, you look just like any other human being! When you come to think of it nobody would believe that we got you from our old red cow. Now Peder, would you like to come home with me and see your mother?' 'I'm afraid I can't,' replied the merchant, 'for I have so much business to attend to.' 'You could take over our farm straight away,' went on the farmer; 'then we two old ones could settle down and enjoy our retirement; but, of course, if you want to carry on with your business that is your affair. Before I go back home is there anything you need?' 'The only thing I'm short of is money,' answered Peder. 'A merchant can always do with that.' 'Just what I thought,' said the farmer; 'poor fellow, you never had any in the first place to help you make a start. Anyhow, don't worry, I've brought plenty with me.' So saying, he untied his money bag and emptied on the table dozens of bright shining florins. Now when the merchant saw how generous his visitor was, he became kind and friendly towards him, and begged him to stay a few days so that they could talk things over. 'Very well,' agreed the farmer, 'but only on condition you call me "father".' 'But both my dear parents are dead,' said the merchant sadly. 'Oh, I know your real father was sold at the cattle-market down in Hamburg last year on St. Michael's Day, and your real mother died when she was calving in the spring, but your mother and I adopted you as a child and, as you are our only heir, you must call me "father".'

Realizing he might benefit by doing so, Peder Okse obeyed, and during the next few days the farmer made out his will, bequeathing to him everything he owned. He then travelled back to his wife, anxious to tell her the good news. How pleased she was to hear that their Peder had been found! 'You must go at once and tell our churchsinger,' she said, 'and don't forget to pay him back the ten pounds we owe him for the books he bought. That is the least we can do to show him our gratitude for teaching Peder and for helping to find him again. It is really through him that we have a son and heir at all.'

The farmer agreed. Along to the churchsinger he went to thank him for all he had done, and he showed his appreciation by giving him twenty pounds instead of the ten pounds he owed. Then he sold his farm, and with his wife he moved to the town where their dear son and heir lived, for they couldn't bear to be so far from him. There they stayed happily until their dying day when Peder Okse inherited all their fortune.

NINETEEN

The Hen with the Golden Legs

ONCE UPON A time there were three sisters who loved each other and their widowed mother very dearly. Riches they had never known, and their only possession was a hen with golden legs. However, the hen was really of no use; although it always went around cluck-clucking, it never laid a single egg for them.

Not far from the house was a big hill, and here the mountain-man lived. As time went by the daughters and their mother became more and more convinced that the hen went up the hill to lay its eggs and that the mountain-man was eating them all. They couldn't be quite sure of this, of course, so one morning the eldest girl said to the youngest, 'I want you to tie a piece of thread round our hen's legs and follow her so that we can find out where she has her nest, for that is where she is bound to go.' The youngest sister did as she was asked and they kept a watch on the hen.

The next day the hen went up the hill to the mountain-man's home where, behind the stove, she laid her eggs. The girl who followed close behind noticed where the hen went, quickly gathered all the eggs and put them in her apron pocket. She was just ready to leave when in came the mountain-man. It was indeed a pleasant surprise for him to find a young girl in his home. He put on his kindest face and in his pleasantest voice said, 'Good morning, my little girl, wouldn't you like to become my maid?' 'No,' replied the girl nervously, 'I was only looking for our hen, and now that I have found her, I'm going home to my mother with the eggs.' 'But you would have a much easier life here,' said the mountain-man; 'all you would have to do would be to make my bed, sweep the floor and spin a pound of flax a day.' The girl didn't like the idea, but the mountain-man was so persuasive that at last she agreed to give it a trial just for one day. Soon the mountain-man had gone and she was left alone. She made his bed, swept the floor and then sat at the spinning-wheel. As she was working away there came a big cat which suddenly jumped on her lap, purred and said, 'Twist it as thick as my tail, as thick as my tail.' 'Off with you, you wretch! It won't turn out very well if I do it as thick as that,' she cried, pushing the cat away. But as fast as she knocked it down, the cat kept jumping up.

When late in the evening the mountain-man returned, he said, 'Good evening, my child. Did you manage to finish your work today?' 'No, I didn't,' replied the girl, 'how could I possibly finish when it had to be done properly?' 'I didn't say it had to be done properly,' said the mountain-man. 'Now come along with me and I'll give you your wages.' Obediently she followed him into the next room and here he cut off her head. That was the only reward she had.

Meanwhile, in their home the two sisters and their mother grew anxious. They went out to look for the little girl, but they searched in vain. All night long they cried until next morning when the mother had an idea. 'You follow the hen today and see whether you can find your sister,' she said to her second daughter. The girl was very frightened but did as her mother asked her. Like her younger sister, she followed the hen to the mountain-man's home and agreed to work for him for one day, the only difference being that she had to spin two pounds of flax instead of one. She, too, scorned the cat's advice to thread the flax as thick as its tail, and when she did not finish spinning before the mountain-man came home, she, too, lost her head.

They were so worried in the girls' home over the disappearance of the two sisters that it was a long time before they could pluck up enough courage to do anything about it. At long last the mother said to her eldest and only remaining daughter, 'My dear, you are quite clever and can look after yourself. Will you go out after the hen this morning and see what you can find out about your sisters?' The eldest daughter was terrified but did her best to conceal her fear, and followed the hen up the hillside. She was just going into the cave behind the hen when she was startled by the sudden appearance of the mountain-man, who said, 'I'm very glad you have come to help me, little one, for I do need a maid so badly.' 'I won't be your maid,' cried the girl; 'I must hurry home to my mother.' 'But I can offer you such a comfortable life,' went on the mountain-man. 'All you have to do is to make my bed, sweep the floor and spin three pounds of flax a day. And who knows, we two might even get married, for I ought to tell you that I am a widower.' At first the girl was unwilling to agree, but the mountain-man seemed so kind and gentle that in the end she was persuaded to stay for just one day. Very contented with himself, the mountain-man went out.

The eldest daughter decided to start with the spinning since she feared she might not finish before he came home. As with her two sisters the cat came and jumped on her lap, purred and said, 'Twist it as thick as my tail, as thick as my tail.' 'That is good advice,' thought the girl, and she proceeded to spin the thread as thick as the cat's tail. In this way she managed to spin all three pounds of flax before the mountain-man came home.

When he returned and saw that the girl had finished all the work he had set her, the mountain-man looked very pleased. 'Good work, my child!' he exclaimed. 'Tomorrow I am going out to shop for our wedding. While I am gone, polish up all the gold and silver and all the furniture, for when we are married everything that is mine shall be yours.'

Next day the girl got up very early for she had much to do. She was busy all morning, but by dinner-time her work was done. In the afternoon, having nothing else to do, she decided to explore the mountain-man's home. She soon came to the closed door and couldn't resist turning the handle. At first it remained fast, but her curiosity got the better of her, and she turned and pulled with all her strength until finally it opened. When she saw the bodies of her two sisters she almost fainted. There was no time to waste, however, and as soon as she had recovered from the shock she quickly put the eggs in her apron and collected as much gold as she could carry. Then she ran off home as fast as she could to tell her mother all that had happened to her.

The fate of her two daughters grieved her mother deeply, and both she and her eldest daughter were sad for many days. However, the old hen with the golden legs brought them some consolation. From then on it never wandered up the hillside, but laid them golden eggs every day; and soon they became very rich. As for the mountain-man, they never heard or saw anything of him since the day the eldest daughter ran away from the cave, for when he returned and found how he had been fooled, his rage was so great that he burnt up with fury.

TWENTY

Master Erik

UP IN VENDSYSSEL there used to live a rich couple. They had eleven sons all of whom were lively and clever. Thus, as soon as they were old enough, their parents encouraged them to go out into the world to seek their fortune. They travelled south to a land where some wicked invaders called Dog-turks were waging war and laying waste the countryside. These fiends had dogs' heads and their food consisted of human flesh. The sons at once gave battle to the Dog-turks and chased them out of the country. The King was so grateful that he gave to each son a princess and a bountiful dowry for saving his country and his people. Now the day before their weddings were to be celebrated, the brothers went riding far into the country. They were pleased with the honour they had earned and talked of nothing else all day long. Too late, they realized the sun had set and that they were lost in the middle of a dark and desolate forest. All they could do was to loosen their reins and hope their horses would lead them home.

It was long past midnight when deep in the forest they saw a light and immediately headed towards it. At last they came to a great cave in the mountainside from which the light shone, and on either side of the entrance stood rows and rows of stones which looked like human beings and horses. Each stone they passed seemed to wave them back and their courage began to fail them. Then, from the entrance of the cave a gruesome-looking troll came out to meet them. Briefly he welcomed them and asked them if they would like to stay for a while inside his hall. They accepted, though their hearts were in their mouths. Each of the brothers would gladly have turned back but none of them wanted to be called a coward. Everything was light and beautiful inside the hall and the tables were brimfull of the richest foods and the choicest wines. The troll himself looked better in this light and he asked them to join him at the table. He was kindness itself and offered them all his fine food and exquisite wine. Glass after glass he gave them, and the more they drank the more beautiful everything appeared. The troll was kindness itself to them and they even called him 'father'. In reply he smiled icily and proposed a toast: 'May you all live with me for ever and may your parents and your past life be forgotten!' The brothers obediently drank the toast with him, but when that was over the troll waved his rune-staff above them and they were turned into stone. Then he hurriedly placed them outside with all the others.

Many years had now passed and the boys' parents had grown old. They prayed that before they died they might see their sons again. The country had been scoured and they had asked everywhere, but their boys could not be found. By this time Svanhvide (Swanwhite), the brothers' young sister, had grown up and decided to go out into the world to search for them. Although her parents, fearing for her safety, begged her not to go, she had made up her mind, and early one morning she set out. Svanhvide wandered southwards, and late one evening arrived at a lonely hut in a distant forest. Here she asked for shelter. The old woman, who had called her inside, sat in the corner by the stove. She welcomed Svanhvide, asked her where she came from and what brought her there. Svanhvide told her of the disappearance of her brothers and of her parents' deep sorrow. 'I suppose you don't know where they might be?' she inquired. The old woman said nothing, but prepared a meal for Svanhvide and bade her eat. She waited until the girl had finished and then said, 'Yes, I know where your brothers are. They are in the mountain with the troll, and you will never be able to reach them for the road is in darkness day and night with deep chasms on either side. Many have tried to reach the troll's home but no one has ever come back.' Hearing this, Svanhvide lost heart and cried at the thought of never being able to see her brothers again. She asked the old woman if she would help her. 'I will,' replied the old woman, 'but even if you do get there you cannot speak to your brothers, for they have been turned into stone. However, if you promise to do exactly as I tell you, I will do all I can for you. Look there, behind the door! That small grey donkey is as old as I am. Get on it and let it go wherever it wants to, and it will take you through the forest to a cave in the mountainside. When you reach the entrance of the cave, get off the donkey and it will come home to me. The soil will be red-hot and even though there are several pairs of shoes lying about, you must walk in your bare feet, otherwise you will not be able to save your brothers. As you come to the door of the hall, you will see eleven stones: these are your brothers. Now take this,' and she reached for a herb from the shelf and handed it to Svanhvide, 'and stroke your brothers with it from head to toe. Then they will come to life again. Off you go, but remember what I said about the shoes!'

Svanhvide thanked the old woman for her kindness, climbed on to the donkey and said good-bye. She rode off hopefully into the night. At first the donkey would do no more than trot, but the farther they travelled the faster it went. Soon they were speeding along the road, over mountains, along valleys, through daylight and darkness. At long last the donkey stopped within sight of the entrance to the mountain that the old woman had described. Svanhvide got off the donkey and at once it turned round and galloped off the way it had come. Then, barefooted, she began walking towards the cave. But everywhere the path was hard and jagged and the stones were sharp and hot. Her poor feet were soon covered with deep cuts and burns, and with every step the road became harder and hotter. She looked longingly at the many pairs of lovely shoes which lined the pathway. 'If only I could put some shoes on, my feet would be saved,' she thought, but then she remembered the old woman's warning, and carefully she carried on. Soon she came within sight of the stones which were her brothers and this gave her fresh heart. At that very moment, however, a black cloud obscured her view. She wanted to run so that she would not lose her brothers in the dark, but the road was now red-hot and she realized that it was impossible to reach her goal without some protection for her feet. She quickly made up her mind and reached for a pair of shoes close by and put them on. Now the road was easy and she was soon beside her brothers. She reached for her herb to stroke them with, but it was gone. Then the troll rushed out of the door towards her. As he waved his rune-staff over her, her hands, her feet and her legs were turned into stone and she couldn't move. But no matter how often the troll swung his rune-staff he could not turn her completely into stone. Finally he shouted, 'Stand there!' And there she stood for many years, singing mournful songs and

Soon she came within sight of the stones . . .

crying sorrowful tears which the troll collected and
stored in a bottle.

The years of waiting were indeed long and hard for
Svanhvide's parents. However, they were not alone, for
soon after their daughter had left, a twelfth son was
born to them. Although he was christened Erik, everyone called him Master Erik. From his early days Erik
learned the meaning of sorrow – sorrow that weighed
heavily in his home and helped him to mature at an
early age. Thus, by the time he was twelve years old, he
was almost a grown man. As a young child he had heard
his parents talking so often of his brothers and sister
whom they supposed to be in the power of the troll, and
even then he had decided that one day he would go out
to rescue them. He dared not mention it to his father
and mother, however, for he was now all they had and
they would break their hearts if he, too, should leave
them. One day, having heard his mother talk of his
brothers and sister, he went out into the forest with his
sword and started chopping away at a huge oak-tree
which had been there for more than a hundred years.
He thought that if he could fell such a tree then the
troll must surely give in to him. For days, weeks, months
and years he chopped, but all in vain. After a hard day's
work he would go home, but when he returned the next
morning he would find the trunk as perfect as when he
had first started. Erik lost heart.

One day when Master Erik was chopping away at
his tree as usual, the trunk suddenly opened and out
popped a little man. 'You're not getting on with your
work very well!' exclaimed the man. 'You've been chopping at my home now for years, and even if you go on
until the end of time you still won't be any nearer finishing.' Erik had not realized until then that his work
might never come to an end, but now the truth dawned

. . . sadly he let his sword sink to the ground.

on him, and sadly he let his sword sink to the ground. 'Yes,' went on the little man, 'I know you have made up your mind first to fell the tree and then to save your brothers, but you will achieve neither in this way. Come out to see me tomorrow and please bring some food, for I haven't eaten for a hundred years. Then I will try to help you.' Erik promised to do as he asked and went home, thinking all the way of the strange little man in the tree.

Early the next morning with a bag of sandwiches in his hand, Erik set off again for the forest. The little man, who was expecting him, greedily swallowed the food, and when he had finished eating, he asked for Erik's old sword. Erik gave it to him, and the old man ran his fingers lightly over the sharp edge. Then, returning the sword to Erik, he said, 'Now see whether you can chop down the old oak.' With all his strength Erik struck the tree once and the old oak fell. 'Now my home has gone,' sighed the old man, 'but remember that I only let you do it because I am fond of you, and now you must promise me that if you kill the troll who has your brothers and sister in thrall, you will give me his home instead.' Erik gave his promise. 'It is time you were on your way,' continued the little man. 'Here is a whistle which you must blow if danger threatens you, and there is my riding-horse. Get on it and it will take you to the troll's home. Now remember this: on your journey you may look round twice, but if you turn round for the third time you will lose your way. When you come to the mountain, do not stay with your brothers and sister but ride straight through to the innermost chamber where the door will open at the touch of your sword. There you will be told what to do next.'

Tying his sword at his hip, Erik went over to the little man's riding-horse which turned out to be a wolf. He jumped on its back and they were off. Before long the wolf was howling terribly and gnashing its teeth. Erik became frightened and couldn't resist looking round. There, closing in on them, was a pack of wolves. Erik was now terrified, but his 'horse' bared its teeth and charged right through them. They were soon clear of the fierce animals and Erik settled down to his ride again. Only for a few miles did they go, however, when a frightful growling and roaring rent the air. Erik was so afraid that he had to turn round, knowing well that this was the last time he could look behind him. All around them were scores of lions and tigers, but the brave wolf fought its way through them. It was now very weary from the struggle and had to go slowly in order to regain its strength; but as the miles went by they gradually gathered speed. Then for the third time the peace of the night was disturbed. There was a howling, a wailing, a roaring and a screeching, and the wolf shot through the air at a breath-taking pace. Worse and worse grew the struggle as hundreds of hideous monsters closed in on them from all sides. The boy thought his end had come and turned round for the third time. Suddenly his 'horse' had gone and a monster grabbed him. Over the sea he was carried and far away. At last the monster tired, and was just going to drop him into the depths below when Erik remembered his whistle. He took it from his pocket and blew it. No sooner had he done so than a huge eagle swooped on to the monster, seized its prey and flew off with Erik on its back.

'Why did you disobey me and look around for the third time?' asked the eagle, and Erik now knew that it was the little man from the forest who had rescued him. 'It was the troll who put all those monsters in your path and it was he, himself, who caught you,' said the bird.

The eagle flew back towards the shore and swooped down in front of the troll's home. Then it said to Erik who had climbed down from its wing, 'Now go straight ahead. I can't follow you any farther until you have done your deed.' Sword in hand, Erik immediately went towards the troll's hall where he saw all the stones and Svanhvide ahead of them, singing her mournful song with the tears rolling down her cheeks. Erik was sorely tempted to stay with her, but then he remembered the little man's words and did not hesitate. Past his brothers and sister he went, and on upstairs to the hall. He was just going to enter when a long, piercing shriek shook the building to its foundations. Erik hurried on until he reached the innermost chamber. Then he touched the door with his sword and it opened wide. In the middle of the room in front of a beautiful young woman knelt the troll, vainly trying to win her favours. Erik dashed straight up to him and thrust the sword through his back. With a terrible yell the troll fell forward; at the same time the young girl fainted and even Erik trembled. Erik quickly recovered, took off his belt and tied it tightly round the troll, who cried, 'Through you my power is broken for ever, so I humbly beg of you to let me stay alive. Ask me what you will, except my life, which cannot harm you now, and you shall have it. After all, you have been lucky, for if you had not found me kneeling and stabbed me from behind, you would never have escaped from here alive.' 'First of all,' said Erik, 'you must tell me how to break the spell you have cast over my brothers and sister. If you refuse I shall light a fire and throw you into it.' 'I won't tell you that,' declared the troll, 'for if they come to life again they will show me no mercy.' Without a word Erik went outside and lit a fire. Then he returned and asked the troll a second time how he might free his brothers and sister. 'I shall never reveal that!' repeated the troll. 'All right, we shall see,' replied Erik, and picking up the troll, he threw him into the fire. The monster struggled to free himself, but the more he wriggled the tighter the belt became. Finally he gave in and shouted, 'Get me out of the fire and I will free your brothers and sister.' 'No,' answered Erik, 'you'll cheat me.' 'Here, round my neck,' screamed the troll, 'is a bottle that I have filled with your sister's tears. If you bathe your brothers and sister with them from head to toe and then let your brothers kiss your sister, the spell will be broken. Now leave me and let me live in peace.' 'No,' said Erik, 'not until everything and everybody under your spell are free. If you refuse, this will be the end of you.'

Erik put some more wood on the fire and the troll groaned and swore. Finally, as the flames licked his face, he shouted, 'Save my life, I am dying. Let me out of the fire. If you go into my room you will see a door in the wall. Touch it with your sword and it will open. Then a bird will fly out and every spell will be broken. Now let me out of the fire quickly or I shall be burnt to death.' 'If it's true what you say I'll spare your life,' said Erik, and he pulled the troll out of the fire, snatched the bottle of tears from his neck and started bathing his brothers and sister. Immediately they came to life, stretched and yawned as though after a long and terrible dream. Erik then kissed his sister and bade his brothers do likewise. Then she, too, was free and they were overjoyed.

But the screaming of the troll made Erik realize there was more for him to do. To the innermost chamber of the hall he went and beat the door in the wall three times with his sword. It opened, and out flew a bird into a near-by tree where it sang very beautifully. Suddenly a mighty whirlwind struck the hall and every-

thing turned upside down. When all was quiet again
they looked around and found themselves in a magnificent palace. In front of them stood a King with his
daughter at his side. The King smiled and said, 'Do you
know me, Master Erik?' But Erik had never seen a King
before in his whole life. He was dazed and puzzled. 'I
am the little man whose tree you chopped down in the
forest,' continued the King. 'The troll, by his magic, had
imprisoned me there because I would not give him my
daughter, and as she refused to marry him, he took my
singing-bird and locked it up. Then he turned my palace
and everybody inside it into stone – that is, everybody
except my daughter whom he kept locked up in a cell;
and every day he tormented her and tried to woo her.'

Down in the courtyard the laughter and singing of
the courtiers and servants who had come back to life
again, filled the air. Horses neighed in their stables,
dogs barked joyfully in their kennels and birds sang
sweetly in their bowers. Through the palace gates
streamed hundreds of the King's subjects who had been
petrified, and among these was the King's only son.
When the King announced that Master Erik was to
have his daughter and Svanhvide was to marry his son,
the prince, a great cheer went up. The double-wedding
was to be celebrated as soon as it could be arranged.
But as he spoke everyone heard the screams of the troll
and a shiver ran through them all. 'I have promised to
free him,' said Erik, 'so I suppose I shall have to keep
my word.' 'No,' they all protested together, 'the troll
must never be freed or we shall suffer a worse fate than
before.' Then they rushed outside and pushed the troll
farther into the fire. 'Oh!' he yelled, 'Erik has promised
me life and you cannot take it from me.' The fire burnt
down and the troll disappeared, but out of the ashes
sprang a fox which dashed through the courtyard off to

the forest. 'You should not have promised him life, Erik,' said the King, 'for then we should finally have been rid of him. Now, as a fox, he will always be snooping around. Still, he will have no power any more, so let us be thankful and make merry. Tomorrow we will come with you to your parents' home.'

We may be quite sure that the old people in their empty home were overjoyed to see all their children again. The double-wedding was proclaimed throughout the country and the celebrations went on for many days. When the feasting was over, Erik, his bride and father-in-law returned to their own magnificent palace; and when eventually the old King died, Master Erik shared the crown and kingdom with Svanhvide and her prince.